Shards of Light

The Eclipse Chronicles, Volume 1

Kenneth Thomas

Published by Kenneth Thomas, 2024.

SHARDS OF LIGHT

First edition. November 17, 2024.

Copyright © 2024 Kenneth Thomas.

ISBN: 979-8230890065

Written by Kenneth Thomas.

Also by Kenneth Thomas

The Awakening Thread Chronicles
The Awakening Thread

The Convergence of Minds series
The Digital Agora: A Philosophical Epic of AI and Humanity
Foundation of the Agora
Beyond the Agora: Fractured Realms

The Eclipse Chronicles
Shards of Light

The Veil of Shadows Series
Shattered Dominion
The Fractured Path

Standalone
A Tail of Darkness To Light

The Mirror Within
Echoes of Ink and Heart
Purpose Over Power: The Visionary Path of Servant Leadership
The Questions That Shape Us: Finding Life's Wisdom-The Power of Inquiry
Where the Shadows Settle
30 Days to Inner Freedom: A Mindful Journey in Addiction Recovery
Towards a Sustainable Future: The UN's 17 Goals
Echoes of Becoming

Table of Contents

Shards of Light
Series: The Eclipse Chronicles
By Kenneth Thomas
Prologue: Fractured Radiance
The world shattered without a sound.

In the Sunlit Chamber at the heart of Solaris Citadel, the Axis Mundi—a perfect sphere of crystalline light that balanced the forces of creation—fractured. There was no explosion, no tremor of stone, only the silent flash of light too bright to behold, an illumination that burned away all certainty.

The radiance rippled outward, spilling through the mirrored dome above the chamber, casting jagged beams into the endless skies. Far below, the gilded spires of Solaris trembled, their reflections refracting the light into kaleidoscopic shards that danced across the golden plains. Within moments, the city's hum of perfection faltered, giving way to an unnatural stillness.

Beneath the shattered Axis, the Sun-Emperor staggered, his golden crown slipping from his head to clatter on the marble floor. He clutched at his chest, where the brilliance of the Axis had seared him, its light now turned to chaos. Around him, the Radiant Order—the priests and scholars who had devoted their lives to the study of light—lay sprawled, blinded by the force of their own faith.

The Emperor's voice cracked as he spoke. "This cannot be."

But it was.

The Axis Mundi, the celestial heart of Ecliptica, was broken. Its shards scattered, flung to the farthest corners of the realms, carrying with them the power to shape the very fabric of existence. And with their fall, the balance between light and shadow—the fragile equilibrium that had governed the world for centuries—collapsed.

Far beneath Solaris, the Umbral Depths stirred.

Selara Veyne stood in the shadowed halls of Chiaroscuro Hollow, her breath catching as the ground trembled beneath her feet. Around her, the towering sculptures of the Depths—carved from obsidian and animated with shadow-magic—shuddered as if alive. The bioluminescent fungi that clung to the cavern walls flickered, casting the chamber in stuttering shades of light and dark.

Selara pressed a hand to her chest, to the shard that rested there, a small fragment of blackened crystal she had found weeks ago in the ruins of a battlefield. At first, it had hummed softly, a quiet resonance that matched the aching rhythm of her grief. Now, it burned, its power flaring in waves that made her fingers tremble.

The air smelled of damp stone and something acrid, like the bite of scorched metal. Selara's eyes darted to her latest creation—a monolithic sculpture that twisted upward, its edges sharp and jagged, a tribute to her lost lover, Laryn. As the shard's energy surged, the sculpture cracked, its base splitting apart. Shadow tendrils erupted from the fissures, curling and writhing with a life of their own.

Selara stumbled back, her heart pounding. She raised a trembling hand, trying to will the shadows into stillness. But they did not obey.

"Stop," she whispered, her voice breaking. "Please."

The shadows only writhed faster, consuming the sculpture in a frenzy of chaotic energy. Selara fell to her knees, the shard's cold pulse reverberating through her chest. For a fleeting moment, she thought she could feel something vast and ancient, reaching through the shadows toward her.

And then it was gone.

In the Twilight Marches, Tavriel sat at the edge of the Eclipsed Ridge, his staff resting across his knees. The skies above the Marches were caught in eternal dusk, painted in gradients of purple and gold. But now, the horizon had dimmed further, as if the light of the sun had faltered.

Tavriel's blind eyes glimmered faintly, their pale irises reflecting the shifting skies. Though he could not see, he felt the fracture as keenly as if it had torn through his own flesh. The shard embedded in his staff thrummed with a low, haunting resonance, vibrating in time with the pulse of the world.

His visions came unbidden. Flickers of potential futures:

A golden city crumbling beneath a shadowed sun.

Sculptures of shadow and light intertwined, forming a figure of terrible beauty.

A lone knight, walking across a burning desert, his shard blazing like a second heart.

And a figure in the distance—neither light nor shadow, yet both—standing at the threshold of something vast.

Tavriel gripped his staff tightly, his knuckles whitening. His voice emerged as a whisper, barely audible above the stillness of the Marches.

"The Axis is undone," he said. "And the Eclipse is rising."

Far from the spires of Solaris and the shadows of the Depths, Kaelion Ashtear trudged through a desert that stretched endlessly beneath an unrelenting sun. His armor, once polished to a mirror's shine, was tarnished and scorched, its golden plating marred by the stains of sand and time. Each step sent a faint crunch echoing through the desolate expanse, the sound swallowed by the oppressive silence of the desert.

At his side, wrapped tightly in a bundle of cloth, the shard pulsed with an icy rhythm. He hadn't meant to take it. It had called to him, humming faintly in the ruins of a village destroyed by the endless war between light and shadow. Now it felt like a brand, a reminder of the guilt he carried and the lives he could not save.

Kaelion paused, lifting his gaze to the horizon. The heat shimmered around him, warping the distant sands into mirages of water and shade. For a moment, the sun dimmed, its blinding light shadowed by something vast and unseen. The shard at his side flared, cold against his hip.

His hand went instinctively to the hilt of his sword, though he knew no blade could cut through what he felt—the wrongness, the fracture, the sense that something essential had been broken.

Kaelion exhaled slowly, his breath rasping in the dry air. "Whatever this is," he murmured, his voice hoarse, "it's not over."

The Axis Mundi was no more, and its shards had scattered across the realms, each carrying a fragment of its immeasurable power. In the days to come, they would awaken those who found them—Kaelion, Selara, Tavriel, and others unknown—transforming them into vessels of light and shadow.

But power was never without cost.

And as the shards began to stir, so too did the forces that sought to claim them. The fragile balance of Ecliptica had been broken, and the age of the Eclipse had begun.

Chapter One: The Exile of Light

The desert stretched endlessly, its sands shimmering like molten gold beneath an unyielding sun. The heat danced in waves, turning the horizon into a mirage of shimmering light and false promise. Kaelion Ashtear trudged through the wasteland, the weight of his armor pressing into his shoulders like a curse.

Each step was a struggle, the crunch of sand beneath his boots a rhythmic reminder of the silence surrounding him. There was no breeze to cool the air, no birds to break the stillness, only the faint metallic scrape of his tarnished sword as it swung against his hip. His mouth was dry, his tongue rough as he tasted the bitter tang of iron that still clung to the back of his throat.

The shard pulsed at his side, wrapped tightly in a bundle of leather and cloth. Its cold energy radiated through the makeshift bindings, a sharp contrast to the oppressive heat. He had found it weeks ago in the ruins of a village, nestled amid ash and shattered stone. Even now, he could hear the faint hum it made, like the whisper of something vast and unknowable.

Kaelion glanced at the horizon, his vision blurred by the sun's relentless glare. Somewhere ahead, the ruins of a forgotten outpost lay buried beneath the sands, a remnant of an age before the Axis divided the realms. It was a place he might rest, if only for a moment.

But rest was a luxury he could ill afford.

The attack came without warning.

Kaelion froze as a faint ripple disturbed the stillness. His hand moved instinctively to the hilt of his sword, the worn leather of its grip familiar against his palm. He scanned the dunes, his gaze narrowing as he caught the glint of metal—a flash of sunlight reflecting off a blade.

Solaris Inquisitors.

They moved like wraiths, their golden armor blending with the desert's glare, their movements precise and unrelenting. There were three of them, their faces hidden behind polished visors, their steps silent as death.

Kaelion's breath caught, his chest tightening as memories clawed their way to the surface. He had once stood among their ranks, sworn to uphold the light of Solaris. Now, he was their prey, an exile hunted for his defiance.

The leader raised a hand, a signal. Kaelion saw the faint shimmer of Solar Relics—their crystalline devices—mounted to their gauntlets, and his grip on his sword tightened. He knew what was coming.

The air ignited as the first blast struck. A beam of concentrated sunlight carved through the sand where Kaelion had stood moments before, the heat searing his skin as he rolled to the side. He came up with his sword drawn, the blade catching the light as he squared off against the advancing Inquisitors.

The second blast was closer, a lance of radiant energy that scorched the ground in a blinding arc. Kaelion raised his blade, deflecting the strike with a grunt of effort. The shard at his side pulsed violently, as if sensing the danger, its cold rhythm quickening to match his heartbeat.

The leader of the Inquisitors stepped forward, his voice amplified by the Resonance Helm that covered his face.

"Kaelion Ashtear," the voice echoed, metallic and hollow. "In the name of the Sun-Emperor, surrender the shard."

Kaelion's jaw tightened. "And if I don't?"

The leader tilted his head, the reflective surface of his visor hiding his expression. "Then you will burn with it."

The fight was swift and brutal.

The first Inquisitor lunged, his blade arcing toward Kaelion's throat. Kaelion sidestepped, the movement fluid despite the weight of his armor, and countered with a strike that glanced off the Inquisitor's shoulder. Sparks flew as steel met steel, the clash ringing sharp and clear against the desert's silence.

The second came from behind, his Solar Relic charging with a high-pitched whine. Kaelion spun, raising his sword just in time to deflect the beam, the force of the impact sending vibrations up his arm.

He could feel the shard's energy coursing through him now, its cold power threading into his veins. It was not the first time it had done this, but it was no less unsettling. The air around him seemed to shift, the sunlight dimming for the briefest moment.

The shard flared.

Kaelion's sword pulsed with light, a radiant glow that burned along its edges. He moved before he could think, his blade cutting through the air with unnatural precision. The first Inquisitor fell, his armor crumpling as Kaelion's strike tore through it.

The second hesitated, his gauntlet raised but unsteady. Kaelion pressed the advantage, his movements a blur as he closed the distance. His sword struck true, and the second Inquisitor dropped to the sand, his Solar Relic flickering out.

Only the leader remained.

The air between them was heavy with tension, the heat of the desert mingling with the shard's cold pulse. The leader raised his blade, its surface shimmering with energy, and for a moment, Kaelion saw himself reflected in the polished metal—a soldier, a knight, a traitor.

"You've fallen far," the leader said, his voice low and edged with contempt.

Kaelion's grip tightened on his sword. "I didn't fall. I chose."

The leader charged, his blade arcing downward in a strike meant to cleave. Kaelion met him head-on, their swords colliding with a crack of light that sent a shockwave rippling through the sands. The shard flared brighter, its energy spilling into Kaelion's limbs as he drove forward, pushing the leader back step by step.

With a final, desperate strike, Kaelion's blade shattered the leader's weapon, sending fragments of glowing metal scattering across the sand. The Inquisitor fell to his knees, his visor cracked, the light within it dimming.

Kaelion stood over him, his chest heaving, the shard's cold pulse beginning to fade.

"You'll never outrun us," the Inquisitor rasped, his voice weaker now. "The light will find you, no matter where you go."

Kaelion turned, his gaze fixed on the horizon. "Then let it find me."

He sheathed his sword and walked away, leaving the Inquisitors broken in the sand.

The sun hung heavy above him as Kaelion continued his journey, the shard at his side pulsing faintly once more. He did not know where he was going, only that he could not stop.

The light had cast him out, the shadow refused to claim him, and the twilight between was waiting.

For the first time in weeks, Kaelion allowed himself a thought: that perhaps the shard's hum was not just a warning, but a call.

And somewhere far away, beneath skies of perpetual dusk, that call would soon be answered.

Chapter Two: The Shadows' Lament

The air in Chiaroscuro Hollow was heavy with the scent of damp stone and the faint, metallic tang of shadow-magic. Selara Veyne stood motionless in her studio, staring at the fractured remains of her latest creation. The sculpture had been a towering monument to Laryn, her lover, now shattered into shards of blackened obsidian and fading wisps of shadow.

Around her, the cavern breathed. The walls pulsed faintly, streaked with veins of bioluminescent fungi that cast a cold, blue glow. The faint hum of shadow-veins echoed through the air, a sound so constant it had become as natural as her own heartbeat. But now, the rhythm of the Hollow felt off—disjointed, chaotic.

It had started hours ago. The shard she carried, a jagged fragment of onyx no larger than her palm, had begun to pulse with a frantic energy. She had felt it in her chest, cold and sharp, like a blade twisting between her ribs. And then the shadows had moved.

Now, her studio was in ruins.

Selara's fingers trembled as she reached toward the shard, which rested on a pedestal at the room's center. It pulsed faintly, casting long, flickering shadows that danced along the curved walls. She hesitated, her breath hitching. Every instinct told her to destroy it, to banish its corruptive whispers from her mind. But she couldn't. The shard called to her, its hum resonating with the ache in her heart.

She closed her eyes, and the memories came.

It had been a year since the Dayborn had raided their border village, a gleaming battalion of Solaris soldiers descending on their shadowed hamlet like a wave of fire. They had called it a purification—a necessary act to cleanse the "taint" of shadow from the land.

Selara had watched helplessly as they burned the studio she had shared with Laryn, their art turned to ash, their shared life reduced to embers. Laryn had fought. He had stood against the soldiers with nothing but his bare hands, his voice raised in defiance as he fell beneath the blazing strikes of their Solar Relics.

The memory was seared into her mind. The heat of the flames. The sharp, acrid stench of burning wood and flesh. The silence that followed.

It was that silence she had tried to fill ever since. With each sculpture she crafted, with each shadow she shaped, she sought to give form to her grief, to make it something she could touch, control, understand. But it was never enough.

The shard pulsed again, louder this time, jolting Selara from her thoughts. She turned sharply, her eyes narrowing as the shadows along the walls began to shift.

They moved unnaturally, curling and stretching toward her like tendrils of smoke caught in a breeze. Her heart pounded, her pulse quickening as the shard's energy surged. She could feel its cold presence threading into her veins, amplifying her emotions, twisting her grief into something darker.

"Stop it," she whispered, her voice trembling. "You don't control me."

The shadows didn't stop. They coiled around her arms, pulling her forward, their touch both cold and searing. Selara gasped, stumbling as the shard's hum grew louder, its rhythm now an urgent, frantic beat.

"No!" she cried, clenching her fists. She concentrated, forcing her will into the shadows. For a moment, they resisted, writhing and twisting against her mental grasp. But then they stilled, their movements slowing, and finally, they obeyed.

Selara exhaled shakily, the tension leaving her body as she regained control. The shadows receded, slithering back into the corners of the room. The shard's hum softened, its energy ebbing, leaving her in the suffocating stillness of the Hollow.

She sank to her knees, her hands trembling. Her breathing came in ragged gasps, her vision blurred by unshed tears.

"What are you doing to me?" she whispered, her voice cracking.

The shard offered no answer, its faint pulse continuing like a distant heartbeat.

A sharp knock at the door broke the silence.

Selara turned, her breath catching as the door creaked open, revealing the familiar figure of Darven Klyre. He stepped into the room with the confidence of someone who had long since stopped asking permission, his dark cloak billowing slightly as he moved.

"Still playing with shadows, I see," Darven said, his voice dripping with sardonic amusement. His sharp features were half-hidden in the Hollow's dim light, but his dark eyes gleamed with something unreadable.

Selara rose unsteadily to her feet, brushing dust from her hands. "What do you want, Darven?"

Darven's gaze swept over the room, lingering on the fractured remains of her sculpture. "Impressive," he said, his tone laced with mockery. "Another masterpiece destroyed. You're making a habit of this."

Selara's jaw tightened. "If you came here to insult me, don't bother. I'm not in the mood."

Darven smirked, leaning casually against the doorframe. "Relax, Sel. I'm here to deliver a message."

Selara crossed her arms, her expression hardening. "From the council?"

He nodded. "They're convening tonight. Something's happening—something big. The shadows are restless, and the seers are muttering about fractures and... light." He said the last word with disdain, as if it left a bad taste in his mouth.

Selara frowned, unease creeping into her chest. "What kind of fractures?"

Darven shrugged, his smirk fading. "They didn't tell me. But whatever it is, they're calling for everyone. Even you."

Selara narrowed her eyes. "Even me? Since when does the council care what I think?"

"Since the shard started singing," Darven said, his tone sharp. He pointed to the pedestal at the room's center, where the shard rested. "They know you've been hiding it, Selara. And they're starting to wonder why."

Her heart sank. She turned her gaze to the shard, its faint pulse suddenly feeling louder, heavier.

"I didn't ask for this," she said quietly.

Darven's expression softened, just for a moment. "None of us did," he said. Then, without another word, he turned and left, the door closing behind him with a dull thud.

Selara stood in silence, her thoughts swirling like the shadows around her.

The council wanted answers, but what could she tell them? That the shard spoke to her in whispers she couldn't understand? That it pulled her deeper into her grief, her anger, her fear? That she was starting to feel like it wasn't just a shard, but a part of her?

She reached for the shard, her fingers brushing its cold, smooth surface.

"I didn't ask for this," she repeated, her voice barely audible.

The shard pulsed in response, its hum steady and unyielding.

In the distance, the great bells of Chiaroscuro Hollow began to toll, their deep, resonant tones echoing through the cavern. It was the council's summons.

Selara straightened, her expression hardening. Whatever the council wanted, whatever the shard was doing to her, she would face it.

Because if there was one thing she had learned in the wake of Laryn's death, it was this:

When the light takes everything, the shadows are all you have left.

Chapter Three: Shards Collide

The oasis was a cruel illusion.

Kaelion Ashtear slowed his pace as the air shimmered ahead of him, the golden sands giving way to a patch of darkened earth. A cluster of gnarled trees stretched their crooked branches toward the sun, their leaves offering only the barest promise of shade. At their roots, a shallow pool reflected the harsh light, its surface trembling faintly in the stillness.

The sight was unnatural. Kaelion had traveled these wastes for weeks, and nothing about this barren land suggested it could nurture life. The shard at his side pulsed faintly as if it, too, sensed something wrong.

He scanned the horizon, his hand instinctively resting on the hilt of his sword. The desert offered no answers, only the sound of his own ragged breathing and the soft crunch of his boots against the sand.

Still, the water called to him.

Selara Veyne crouched at the edge of the pool, her reflection staring back at her in broken fragments.

The water was clear, unnaturally so, and it mirrored her face with an almost painful clarity. Her violet eyes were rimmed with exhaustion, her pale skin streaked with soot and shadow residue. She had traveled all night to escape the suffocating tension of Chiaroscuro Hollow, the shard's restless hum driving her to the surface.

Now, as she gazed into the pool, the shard around her neck pulsed, its rhythm matching the pounding of her heart. She touched the onyx fragment absently, her fingers tracing its jagged edges.

"Why did you bring me here?" she whispered. The question wasn't for the shard. It was for the shadows that had guided her steps, pulling her toward the desert's edge like a tide.

The pool offered no answer, but the shard flared suddenly, its energy surging through her veins. Selara gasped, stumbling back as the water rippled violently. A shadow flickered across its surface, dark and sharp, and she turned sharply to face the intruder.

Kaelion froze as he reached the edge of the oasis.

The figure before him was unlike anything he'd expected. A woman, clad in shadowed robes, stood at the pool's edge. Her hair, dark as midnight, framed a face that seemed carved from porcelain, though her expression was hard and wary. Around her neck hung a shard—a twin to the one bound at Kaelion's side.

It pulsed faintly, echoing the rhythm of his own.

Their gazes met, the air between them growing taut with tension. Kaelion's hand tightened on his sword, and the woman's fingers flexed as tendrils of shadow coiled around her feet like living things.

"Who are you?" Kaelion demanded, his voice hoarse.

The woman tilted her head, her violet eyes narrowing. "I could ask you the same thing," she said, her tone sharp. "But I'm more interested in why you're carrying that." Her gaze flicked to the bundle at his side, her voice laced with disdain.

Kaelion's heart quickened. She knew. Somehow, she knew about the shard.

"That's none of your concern," he said carefully, his tone low and steady. "Just step aside, and there won't be any trouble."

The woman let out a bitter laugh, her hands clenching into fists. "Trouble? That thing you're carrying is trouble." Her shard flared suddenly, its energy spilling into the shadows around her. "And I'm not stepping aside until I know what you're doing with it."

The pulse of Kaelion's shard grew stronger, its energy crackling like static beneath his skin. He drew his sword, its tarnished blade glinting faintly in the sun. "I'm not looking for a fight," he said. "But if you don't stand down—"

The ground beneath them shuddered.

The shards reacted violently, their energies colliding in a burst of light and shadow.

Kaelion staggered as his shard flared to life, the bundle at his side unraveling as the fragment within unleashed its power. A brilliant, radiant glow erupted from the shard, clashing with the dark tendrils that writhed from the woman's pendant.

Selara cried out, her knees buckling as the onyx shard burned against her chest. She felt its energy lashing out, twisting her control of the shadows into something wild and feral. The tendrils surged forward, colliding with the radiant force of Kaelion's shard in a violent explosion that sent them both sprawling.

The pool at their feet rippled violently, the water boiling away as the shards' energies tore through the oasis. The gnarled trees groaned, their branches splitting and cracking under the strain.

Kaelion scrambled to his feet, his sword raised defensively as Selara rose unsteadily, her breath coming in short, ragged bursts.

"What are you?" he asked, his voice edged with both fear and curiosity.

Selara glared at him, her fingers brushing the shard at her neck. "Someone who knows what those things can do," she said. "And someone who's not about to let you destroy everything with yours."

Kaelion frowned, his grip tightening on his sword. "I didn't choose this. The shard—" He stopped himself, his jaw clenching. "I don't owe you an explanation."

Selara's lips twisted into a bitter smile. "No, you don't," she said. "But you do owe the world an answer. Those shards... they're not meant to exist like this."

The shard at Kaelion's side pulsed faintly, its energy less volatile now but no less present. He took a cautious step forward, lowering his sword slightly.

"If you know what these are," he said slowly, "then maybe you know what to do with them."

Selara's expression darkened. "You think there's a solution to this?" She gestured to the shattered remnants of the oasis around them, the ground scorched and twisted by the shards' collision. "This isn't something you fix. It's something you survive."

Her words hung in the air, heavy and cold.

Kaelion hesitated, his eyes searching hers. There was anger there, yes, but beneath it, there was something else—pain, loss, a grief he recognized all too well.

Before he could respond, a sound broke the silence—a low, guttural growl that seemed to rise from the earth itself.

The ground trembled again, and from the shadows of the broken trees, shapes began to emerge. They moved with an unnatural fluidity, their forms indistinct, flickering between solidity and smoke. Their eyes glowed faintly, reflecting the shards' chaotic energy.

Kaelion raised his sword, his body tensing. "What are those?"

Selara's breath caught as she recognized the creatures for what they were: shadow-forms, summoned by the shards' power. She had seen them before in her studio, fragile and fleeting. But these were different—stronger, more focused.

"Trouble," she said grimly.

The first shadow-form lunged, its elongated limbs slicing through the air like blades. Kaelion sidestepped, his sword flashing as he struck, the radiant energy of his shard burning through the creature's form. It dissolved with a hiss, its remains scattering like ash.

Another charged at Selara, its movements erratic and feral. She raised her hand instinctively, and the shadows around her surged, forming a barrier that deflected the attack. The creature snarled, retreating before lunging again.

The two fought side by side, their movements uncoordinated but effective. Kaelion's sword carved through the shadow-forms with brutal efficiency, while Selara wielded her shard's power with precision, binding the creatures in tendrils of darkness before crushing them.

When the last of the shadow-forms fell, the oasis was silent once more.

Kaelion lowered his sword, his chest heaving. He turned to Selara, his expression wary but less hostile.

"Looks like we both have trouble," he said.

Selara nodded, brushing a strand of hair from her face. "And it's not going away anytime soon."

Kaelion hesitated, then extended a hand. "We need answers. And it seems like you know more than I do. Truce?"

Selara regarded him for a moment, her eyes searching his. Finally, she reached out and took his hand.

"For now," she said.

The shards at their sides pulsed faintly, their energies settling into an uneasy harmony.

Chapter Four: Echoes of the Past

The desert gave way to jagged cliffs, their sunbaked stone carved into natural spires that rose like forgotten sentinels. The air here was cooler, shaded by the uneven peaks, though it carried the dry, metallic tang of scorched rock. Kaelion led the way, his boots crunching against the gravel-strewn path, while Selara followed a few paces behind, her eyes scanning their surroundings with practiced wariness.

Neither had spoken since they left the ruined oasis.

The shard at Kaelion's side had gone quiet, its pulse reduced to a faint thrum, but its presence lingered in his thoughts. He could feel its weight in every step, like a second heart beating against his side, cold and unrelenting.

Selara broke the silence first.

"You're not much of a talker, are you?"

Kaelion glanced over his shoulder, his expression unreadable. "Doesn't seem like there's much to say."

"There's always something to say," she replied. "Like why you're carrying a shard you clearly don't understand."

Kaelion stopped abruptly, turning to face her. His shadow stretched long against the uneven ground, the dimming sunlight casting an amber glow over his weathered armor.

"And what do you understand about it?" he asked, his tone sharp.

Selara met his gaze, her violet eyes steady. "Enough to know it's dangerous." She tapped the onyx shard hanging around her neck, its edges gleaming faintly. "Enough to know these things aren't just relics. They're alive, in their own way."

Kaelion frowned, his hand brushing the cloth-wrapped shard at his side. "Alive?"

Selara nodded. "They respond to us—our emotions, our thoughts. The more you let it into your mind, the harder it is to control." She paused, her voice softening. "The harder it is to stay yourself."

Kaelion's grip tightened on the shard's wrappings. "What makes you think I'm not in control?"

Selara tilted her head, a faint smirk playing at her lips. "Your shard nearly burned down that entire oasis. That doesn't exactly scream 'control.'"

Kaelion bristled but said nothing. He turned and resumed walking, his movements stiff and deliberate.

The cliffs opened into a narrow canyon, its walls streaked with veins of quartz that caught the fading light, refracting it into faint rainbows. The sound of running water echoed faintly from somewhere ahead, the promise of a stream hidden among the rocks.

Kaelion paused at the canyon's mouth, his gaze narrowing.

"Do you hear that?" he asked.

Selara stopped beside him, her brow furrowing. The faint sound of voices drifted through the canyon, carried on the breeze. They were distant, muffled, but unmistakably human.

"We're not alone," she said.

Kaelion's hand went instinctively to the hilt of his sword. "Stay close," he muttered, moving forward with measured steps.

The voices grew clearer as they advanced, echoing off the canyon walls in overlapping bursts of conversation. They rounded a bend and found themselves facing a group of travelers gathered near the stream.

There were four of them, dressed in a patchwork of worn robes and leather armor. Their weapons rested nearby, though within easy reach, and their faces were tense with the wary caution of those who had learned to survive in a harsh world.

One of them, a tall man with a scar running down the side of his face, stepped forward as Kaelion and Selara approached. His hand hovered near the hilt of his blade, though he didn't draw it.

"Travelers?" the man asked, his voice rough. "Or trouble?"

"Depends on how you answer," Kaelion replied evenly. "What are you doing out here?"

The man exchanged a glance with his companions before responding. "We're heading north, to the Marches. Safer roads, fewer raids." His eyes flicked to the bundle at Kaelion's side, then to the shard around Selara's neck. "But it looks like you've brought trouble with you."

Selara stepped forward, her gaze sharp. "These are our burden, not yours."

The man's expression darkened. "Burden or not, those shards bring ruin. We've seen what they can do. If you're carrying one, you're a danger to everyone around you."

Kaelion stiffened, his jaw tightening. "We're not looking for a fight."

"Good," the man said. "Because if you were, it'd be the last thing you found."

The tension between them hung thick in the air, and for a moment, it seemed like a fight was inevitable. But before either side could act, a tremor rippled through the ground, sending loose stones tumbling from the canyon walls.

The stream began to bubble and hiss as a wave of unnatural heat surged through the canyon. Kaelion turned sharply, his sword drawn, as the travelers scrambled for their weapons.

From the shadows of the cliffs, something emerged.

The creature was unlike anything Kaelion had ever seen—a twisted amalgamation of light and shadow, its form shifting and unstable. Its body glowed faintly, veins of molten gold running through its translucent flesh, while tendrils of darkness writhed from its limbs like living smoke.

The travelers shouted in alarm, their weapons raised. The creature let out a soundless roar, its maw splitting open to reveal a void of shimmering energy. It lunged toward the nearest traveler, moving with an unnatural speed.

Kaelion acted on instinct. He charged forward, his sword arcing through the air as the shard at his side flared with energy. The blade struck the creature's limb, severing one of its shadowy tendrils. It recoiled, its body rippling with light and shadow as it turned its attention to him.

Selara stepped in beside him, her shard glowing as she summoned a wall of shadows to block the creature's next attack. The tendrils lashed against the barrier, hissing as they dissolved into smoke.

"It's a shard-beast," she said, her voice taut. "It's drawn to the energy. We have to take it down before it tears this canyon apart."

Kaelion nodded, his focus narrowing to the fight. The travelers joined in, their blades striking at the creature's shifting form, though their attacks seemed to have little effect.

Selara extended her hands, the shadows coiling around her fingers as she sent them lancing toward the creature. The tendrils wrapped around its limbs, holding it in place long enough for Kaelion to drive his blade into its core. The shard's light erupted from the sword, burning through the creature's body in a brilliant explosion.

When the light faded, the creature was gone, its remains scattered as faint motes of energy that dissolved into the air.

The canyon fell silent once more.

Kaelion lowered his sword, his breaths coming in ragged gasps. He turned to Selara, who stood with her hands still raised, her face pale but steady.

"That's twice now," he said. "You saved my life."

Selara gave him a faint smile. "Don't get used to it."

One of the travelers stepped forward, his expression a mixture of awe and fear. "You two... you destroyed it."

Kaelion sheathed his sword, his gaze hard. "We didn't destroy it. The shards did."

The man hesitated, then nodded slowly. "Then maybe... maybe you can survive carrying them. But if you're heading to the Marches, you'll need more than those shards to survive what's waiting for you there."

Kaelion and Selara exchanged a glance, the weight of his words sinking in.

"Then we'd better get moving," Kaelion said.

They turned and continued down the canyon, the travelers' warnings echoing in their minds.

Chapter Five: Whispers of the Codex

The Twilight Marches stretched out before them, a vast expanse of rolling hills bathed in perpetual dusk. The skies were painted in muted hues of purple and gold, streaked with faint tendrils of silver clouds that hung low and heavy. The air here was cool, a welcome reprieve from the searing desert they had left behind, but it carried a faint hum—a sound that seemed to come from nowhere and everywhere at once.

Kaelion Ashtear and Selara Veyne walked in silence, the weight of their journey settling heavily between them. The shard at Kaelion's side pulsed faintly, matching the rhythm of his footsteps, while Selara's hung around her neck, its faint glow casting eerie shadows on her pale skin.

"It feels... different here," Kaelion said, breaking the silence.

Selara nodded, her gaze scanning the horizon. "The Marches are caught between realms. Light and shadow don't hold sway here, not entirely. It's... liminal."

Kaelion frowned. "Liminal?"

Selara glanced at him, her lips curving into a faint smirk. "A place in between. Neither one thing nor the other. Like twilight itself."

He considered this, his gaze lingering on the distant hills. There was a stillness to the Marches, a quiet that felt both soothing and unnerving, as if the land itself was holding its breath.

Ahead, the faint outline of a camp came into view—a cluster of tents arranged in a loose circle around a central fire. The glow of the flames flickered faintly, its light dancing across the fabric of the tents.

Kaelion's hand went to the hilt of his sword as they approached, his movements slow and deliberate. Selara raised a hand, signaling him to wait.

"These are Twilight nomads," she said. "They won't attack us. Not without reason."

"And if they have a reason?" Kaelion asked.

"Then you'd better be quick with that sword," Selara replied dryly.

The camp was smaller than it had appeared from a distance, no more than a dozen tents arranged haphazardly around the fire. The nomads were a mix of ages, their skin weathered by the elements, their clothing a patchwork of fabrics dyed in twilight hues.

An older woman stepped forward as Kaelion and Selara entered the camp, her posture straight despite the weight of years evident in her lined face. Her hair was streaked with silver, and she carried a staff adorned with carvings of crescent moons and interwoven spirals.

"You walk under the skies of the Marches," the woman said, her voice low and measured. "What brings you to this place?"

Kaelion hesitated, glancing at Selara. She stepped forward, her tone calm but firm. "We're travelers, seeking passage through the Marches. We mean no harm."

The woman's gaze shifted to the shards they carried, her expression unreadable. "Travelers, perhaps. But no ordinary ones. The Axis's mark clings to you."

Kaelion stiffened. "You know about the shards?"

The woman nodded slowly. "We know more than you might think. The shards are not yours to wield lightly. They are pieces of a greater whole—a broken truth that should never have been touched."

Kaelion frowned, the woman's words stirring a sense of unease. "Then why haven't you taken them from us?"

"Because it is not our place," she said. "The shards choose their bearers, for better or worse. But if you seek to carry their burden, you must understand what it is you hold."

The woman led them to the central fire, where the other nomads gathered in silence. They sat in a loose circle, their faces illuminated by the flickering flames, their eyes reflecting a quiet intensity.

The woman gestured for Kaelion and Selara to sit, and they complied, though Kaelion kept his hand near his sword.

"The shards," the woman began, her voice carrying the weight of a story often told, "are fragments of the Axis Mundi—the heart of Ecliptica. It is the source of all balance, the thread that binds light and shadow, creation and destruction."

She paused, her gaze distant. "When the Axis shattered, it unleashed chaos upon the realms. The shards carry its power, but also its burden. They amplify what is within—your fears, your desires, your truths. And they demand much in return."

Selara's hand went to the shard at her neck, her fingers brushing its smooth surface. "What does the Axis want?" she asked softly.

The woman's eyes flicked to hers. "It wants to be whole again. But to restore the Axis is not a simple task. The balance it represents is not something that can be forced. It must be earned."

Kaelion frowned. "And how are we supposed to do that?"

The woman's gaze turned sharp. "The answer lies in the Stellar Codex."

The name stirred something deep in Kaelion, a memory buried beneath layers of guilt and regret. He had heard whispers of the Codex during his time in Solaris, tales of a text that held the secrets of creation itself.

"The Codex is real?" he asked, his voice low.

"It is," the woman said. "And it is said to hold the key to restoring the Axis. But the Codex is not a simple guide. It is a reflection, a mirror of the reader's soul. Its truths are elusive, shaped by your intentions and your flaws."

Selara frowned. "And where is this Codex?"

The woman's expression darkened. "That is a question many have sought to answer. Some say it lies hidden in the Eclipsed Ridge, where the shards' resonance is strongest. Others believe it exists only in the mind, revealed through the bearer's journey."

Kaelion and Selara exchanged a glance, the weight of her words sinking in.

"Your journey will not be easy," the woman continued. "The shards will test you. The Codex will challenge you. And there are those who would see you fail—who would claim the shards for themselves."

Kaelion nodded, his resolve hardening. "Then we'll find the Codex. And we'll restore the Axis."

The woman studied him for a long moment, her expression inscrutable. Finally, she rose, her staff tapping against the ground as she stepped away from the fire.

"Then may the twilight guide your steps," she said, her voice soft. "But remember this: the balance you seek cannot be forced. It must be found, within yourself and within the world."

That night, Kaelion and Selara camped at the edge of the nomads' territory, the glow of the central fire a distant flicker on the horizon. The Marches stretched out around them, vast and unknowable, their silence broken only by the faint hum of the shards.

Kaelion sat by their small fire, staring into the flames as the woman's words echoed in his mind. The Codex, the shards, the Axis—it all felt impossibly large, a burden he was not sure he could carry.

"You're thinking too loudly," Selara said, her voice cutting through the quiet.

Kaelion glanced at her, his brow furrowing. "What does that mean?"

Selara smirked faintly, her eyes reflecting the firelight. "It means I can hear you brooding all the way over here."

He sighed, shaking his head. "Do you ever stop being irritating?"

"Not when it's this much fun," she replied.

Despite himself, Kaelion let out a soft chuckle. For a moment, the weight of their journey seemed lighter, the darkness of the Marches less suffocating.

But as he lay down to rest, the shard at his side pulsed faintly, its hum laced with whispers he couldn't quite understand.

The road ahead was long, and the shadows were closing in.

Chapter Six: Shadows at the Gate

The Eclipsed Ridge loomed on the horizon, its jagged silhouette framed by the eternal dusk of the Twilight Marches. The closer they drew, the more the air seemed to hum, a low, resonant vibration that settled into Kaelion's chest like a second heartbeat.

He adjusted the bundle at his side, the shard's pulse growing stronger with each step. Selara walked beside him, her shard glowing faintly at her throat, casting fractured shadows across her face.

"You feel it too, don't you?" she asked, her voice breaking the uneasy silence.

Kaelion nodded. "The shards... they're resonating with something."

"The Ridge," Selara said. Her gaze lingered on the craggy peaks ahead, their surfaces veined with faint streaks of silver and black. "This place is old. Older than the realms themselves. It's no wonder the shards are stirring."

Kaelion's jaw tightened. The weight of the shard pressed against him, its cold energy threading into his veins like ice water. He could feel its influence, subtle but insistent, nudging at the edges of his thoughts.

They crested a rise and saw it—a gate carved into the mountainside, its surface etched with intricate patterns of light and shadow interwoven. The stone shimmered faintly, the engravings shifting as if alive.

Selara's steps slowed, her eyes narrowing. "That's no ordinary gate."

Kaelion stopped beside her, his hand resting on the hilt of his sword. "What is it?"

"Something tied to the shards," she said. "Look at the patterns. They match the resonance marks on the fragments."

Before Kaelion could respond, the air around them shifted, growing heavy with an unseen presence. The hum of the shards grew louder, their pulses quickening.

And then, the shadows moved.

Figures emerged from the Ridge, their forms flickering like distorted reflections on water. They were humanoid, but wrong—too tall, too thin, their limbs elongated and jagged. Their eyes glowed faintly, a pale light that pierced the dusk.

Kaelion drew his sword, its blade catching the faint gleam of the gate's light. "What are they?"

"Shades," Selara said, her voice tight. She raised her hands, shadows coiling around her fingers. "Manifestations of the shards' power. They're not alive, but they'll kill us all the same."

The first shade lunged, its movements unnaturally fast. Kaelion met it head-on, his sword slicing through its translucent form. The blade passed through with a burst of light, and the creature dissolved into ash.

Another came from the side, its claws raking through the air. Kaelion spun, parrying the strike with a grunt of effort. The shard at his side flared, its energy spilling into his limbs, sharpening his movements.

Selara stepped back, her shard glowing as she summoned a wave of shadows. The tendrils lashed out, ensnaring one of the shades and pulling it to the ground. She clenched her fists, and the shadows constricted, crushing the creature into nothingness.

"They're drawn to the shards," Selara said, her voice strained. "The closer we get to the gate, the more there will be."

Kaelion glanced toward the entrance, now only a few paces away. The hum of the shards was deafening, their resonance creating an almost physical pressure. "We can't stop now. If the Codex is here, we need to reach it."

Another shade lunged, its claws aimed at Selara's throat. She turned, her eyes narrowing as the shadows surged to meet the attack, but the creature was faster.

Kaelion moved without thinking. His blade arced through the air, striking the shade with a flash of light that sent it recoiling. It hissed, its form flickering before it vanished into the dusk.

Selara's breath caught, her eyes wide as she looked at him. "You—"

"We don't have time for gratitude," Kaelion said, his tone brusque. "Move."

They pushed forward, cutting through the shades with brutal efficiency. Each strike of Kaelion's sword sent ripples of energy through the air, the shard's power amplifying his movements. Selara's shadows wove around them, striking and binding with precision, her control growing more fluid with each attack.

At last, they reached the gate. The engravings on its surface pulsed in time with the shards, their patterns shifting into a complex, interwoven design. The air around it was thick with energy, a palpable tension that made Kaelion's skin crawl.

Selara reached out, her fingers brushing the surface of the gate. The moment she touched it, her shard flared brightly, and the patterns on the stone shifted, forming a spiral that seemed to draw her in.

"It's reacting to the shards," she said, her voice tinged with awe.

Kaelion stepped closer, his gaze fixed on the spiral. The hum of his shard grew louder, its energy surging through him. For a moment, he hesitated, the weight of the moment pressing down on him.

"What happens if we open it?" he asked.

Selara looked at him, her expression unreadable. "We find out if we're ready for what's on the other side."

With a deep breath, Kaelion placed his hand on the gate. The shards' resonance reached a crescendo, their pulses merging into a single, harmonic tone that filled the air. The engravings glowed brightly, the spiral twisting inward as the gate began to shift.

A faint rumble echoed through the Ridge as the stone split apart, revealing a darkened passage beyond. The air inside was cool and still, carrying the faint scent of earth and something ancient—something alive.

Kaelion stepped through the threshold, his sword at the ready, Selara close behind. The passage descended sharply, its walls lined with the same shifting patterns as the gate. The hum of the shards faded slightly, replaced by an eerie silence that pressed against their senses.

At the end of the passage, they found themselves in a vast chamber. The ceiling stretched high above, its surface adorned with constellations of glowing symbols that pulsed faintly. At the center of the room stood a pedestal, and atop it rested a single object.

The Stellar Codex.

It was not a book, as Kaelion had expected, but a shifting prism of light and shadow, its surface constantly in flux. The patterns within it twisted and turned, forming shapes and symbols that defied comprehension.

Selara stepped forward, her breath catching. "This is it," she whispered. "The Codex."

Kaelion's grip on his sword tightened as he approached the pedestal. The shards at their sides pulsed faintly, their energies aligning with the Codex's shifting rhythm.

But before he could reach out, a voice echoed through the chamber.

"You are not the only ones who seek the truth."

They turned sharply, their weapons raised, as a figure stepped from the shadows. His form was wreathed in both light and darkness, his face obscured by a helm that gleamed like molten gold.

"Lord Cyrix," Selara breathed, her voice filled with dread.

The figure's gaze fell on the Codex, then on them. "The shards have chosen poorly," he said, his tone cold and commanding. "But no matter. The Codex will be mine."

Kaelion raised his sword, his jaw tightening. "Over my dead body."

Cyrix's helm tilted slightly, as though he were smiling. "If that is your wish."

The shards pulsed violently, their energies flaring as the chamber filled with the sound of clashing power.

And the fight began.

Chapter Seven: The Codex Unveiled

The air inside the chamber pulsed with energy, the hum of the shards rising to an almost deafening crescendo. Kaelion's grip tightened on his sword as he faced Lord Cyrix, the enigmatic figure who now stood between them and the Stellar Codex. The faint glow of the Codex bathed the room in shifting light, its presence a constant reminder of the stakes.

Cyrix moved like a shadow caught in the glow of a flickering flame, his form cloaked in a mantle that shimmered with the interplay of light and darkness. His helm obscured his features, but the weight of his gaze was palpable, a pressure that seemed to pierce through Kaelion's defenses.

"You're a long way from Solaris, knight," Cyrix said, his voice a cold, resonant echo. "How far does guilt drive you, I wonder?"

Kaelion's jaw tightened, but he didn't rise to the bait. "You talk too much," he said, leveling his sword.

Cyrix tilted his head slightly. "And you've learned too little."

The shards flared.

Cyrix struck first.

A wave of energy erupted from his outstretched hand, a collision of radiant light and writhing shadow that surged across the chamber. Kaelion dove to the side, the blast shattering the stone where he had stood moments before. Selara moved in tandem, her shadows coiling around her as she countered with a blast of her own, the tendrils lashing out toward Cyrix like living whips.

The clash of power filled the chamber, each strike sending ripples through the air. Kaelion charged, his sword glowing faintly as the shard at his side pulsed in rhythm with his movements. He swung in a wide arc, aiming for Cyrix's midsection, but the other man moved with inhuman speed, his form dissolving into shadow before reforming a few paces away.

"You think brute force will suffice?" Cyrix taunted, his voice cold. "You carry fragments of the Axis, yet you wield them like toys."

Kaelion didn't respond. He pressed forward, his strikes precise and relentless. Cyrix deflected each blow with an almost casual grace, his movements fluid and unhurried.

Selara joined the fray, her shadows weaving around Cyrix in a tightening web. For a moment, it seemed as though they had him trapped. But Cyrix raised his hands, and a burst of radiant energy shattered the web, sending Selara stumbling back.

Kaelion lunged, his blade aimed for Cyrix's exposed side, but Cyrix caught the sword with his gauntleted hand. Light and shadow flared where their weapons met, the shards' energies clashing violently.

"You don't understand what you're fighting for," Cyrix said, his voice low and menacing. "You think the Codex will give you answers? It will give you nothing but pain."

Kaelion's eyes burned with determination. "I've lived with pain. I'll manage."

With a surge of strength, he broke free, forcing Cyrix back.

Selara regrouped, her breath coming in short, ragged gasps. The shard at her neck pulsed erratically, its energy feeding her shadows but draining her strength. She glanced at Kaelion, who was holding his ground against Cyrix, and then at the Codex, its shifting light drawing her gaze.

The Codex pulsed faintly, its rhythm in sync with her shard. A thought flickered through her mind, unbidden but undeniable: the Codex was calling to her.

"Keep him busy!" she shouted to Kaelion.

Kaelion spared her a brief glance, his expression hardening. "What are you doing?"

"Finding out if he's right," Selara said, her voice grim.

She moved toward the Codex, her steps unsteady but determined. The pedestal seemed to glow brighter as she approached, the patterns within the Codex shifting faster, forming symbols and shapes that danced just beyond comprehension.

As her hand neared the Codex, a surge of energy erupted from its surface, forcing her back. She stumbled, her shard flaring brightly in response. The room seemed to dim for a moment, the light from the Codex intensifying, as if testing her resolve.

Selara gritted her teeth and stepped forward again, her fingers brushing the surface of the Codex.

The world fell away.

Selara stood in a void, surrounded by a swirling vortex of light and shadow. The shard at her neck pulsed in time with the rhythm of the Codex, its energy threading into her mind. Images flashed before her—fractured glimpses of past, present, and future:

Kaelion kneeling in a field of ash, his hands stained with blood.

The Sun-Emperor standing before the shattered Axis, his crown gleaming like fire.

A city of shadow and light, its towers crumbling as the sky burned.

And a figure, faceless and vast, standing at the center of it all.

The voice of the Codex whispered through her mind, its tone both soothing and terrifying.

"Balance is not found in what you take. It is found in what you give."

Selara gasped as the vision shifted, the vortex pulling her deeper. She felt the shard's energy intertwining with her own, amplifying her fears and desires. The Codex was showing her something, but the meaning eluded her, slipping through her grasp like sand.

Back in the chamber, Cyrix turned sharply, his attention drawn to Selara.

"No!" he shouted, his voice filled with fury. He moved toward her, his hand outstretched, but Kaelion intercepted him, his blade striking with renewed force.

"You're not getting to her," Kaelion growled, his strikes relentless.

Cyrix snarled, his calm demeanor cracking. "You're playing with forces you don't understand!"

"Then explain them," Kaelion said, driving him back step by step.

Cyrix deflected another strike, his movements growing more erratic. "You think the Codex will save you? It will destroy you! The Axis demands sacrifice. Balance always comes at a cost."

Selara's hand trembled as she withdrew it from the Codex. The chamber came rushing back into focus, the sounds of battle ringing in her ears.

Kaelion and Cyrix were locked in a fierce exchange, their shards flaring with each strike. The Codex pulsed brightly, its patterns shifting into a spiral that seemed to point toward Selara.

She stepped forward, her voice cutting through the chaos. "The Codex... it's not just a key. It's a test."

Kaelion glanced at her, his expression questioning. "A test for what?"

"For us," Selara said, her voice steady despite the tremor in her hands. "To see if we're ready to bear the cost of balance."

Cyrix turned to her, his eyes blazing beneath his helm. "And what makes you think you are?"

Selara met his gaze, her own shard flaring with defiance. "Because I've already paid it."

The chamber fell silent for a moment, the tension thick enough to cut. The shards pulsed in unison, their energies converging on the Codex.

The spiral began to glow brighter, its light spilling across the room, and the Codex shifted once more, its voice echoing faintly.

"The path begins here."

The light consumed them.

Chapter Eight: Fragments of Truth

The light faded, leaving behind an eerie silence.

Kaelion blinked against the sudden dimness, his vision adjusting to the faint glow of the chamber. Selara stood a few paces ahead of him, her hand still outstretched toward the Codex. The air around them was thick, charged with an energy that seemed to hum beneath their skin.

Cyrix was gone.

Kaelion lowered his sword, his breath coming in short, sharp bursts. "What just happened?"

Selara didn't answer immediately. Her gaze was fixed on the Codex, its shifting surface now calm, its light a steady, pulsing rhythm. She turned slowly, her expression unreadable.

"The Codex showed me something," she said, her voice quiet but firm. "Visions. Fragments of what's to come—and what's already been."

Kaelion frowned. "And Cyrix?"

"He's not gone," she replied, her tone grim. "The Codex didn't kill him. It... rejected him."

Kaelion's grip tightened on the hilt of his sword. "Rejected?"

Selara nodded. "He's unworthy. The Codex responds to intent, to the balance within. Cyrix... he's too fractured, too consumed by his own desires."

Kaelion glanced at the Codex, its light reflecting faintly in his tarnished armor. "And us? Are we worthy?"

Selara's gaze met his, a flicker of uncertainty in her eyes. "That remains to be seen."

The chamber shifted around them.

The walls, once adorned with constellations of glowing symbols, began to ripple like water, the patterns flowing into new shapes. The air grew colder, carrying a faint, metallic tang that reminded Kaelion of the shards.

"It's changing," Selara said, her voice tinged with unease. "The Codex is... reacting."

Kaelion stepped closer to her, his sword raised defensively. "To what?"

Before she could answer, the light of the Codex flared, casting the chamber in blinding brilliance. When it dimmed, the room was no longer empty.

Figures surrounded them, translucent and shifting, their forms carved from light and shadow. They hovered in place, their faces indistinct, their movements slow and deliberate.

Selara's breath caught. "Are they... illusions?"

One of the figures stepped forward, its presence radiating a quiet power. Its voice, soft and melodic, filled the chamber.

"We are echoes," it said, its words resonating in the air. "Fragments of the Axis's memory."

Kaelion exchanged a glance with Selara, his unease growing. "Memories?"

The figure nodded, its head tilting slightly. "When the Axis fractured, so too did its knowledge. We are the remnants, bound to the shards and the Codex, awaiting those who would seek the truth."

Selara stepped forward cautiously. "What truth?"

"The nature of balance," the echo replied. "And the price it demands."

The Codex flared again, and the chamber dissolved into a new vision.

Kaelion and Selara stood on a barren plain, the ground cracked and blackened as if scorched by fire. Above them, the sky was split in two—one half bathed in searing light, the other cloaked in impenetrable shadow. The horizon trembled, the two forces colliding in violent bursts of energy.

"This is the cost of imbalance," the echo said, its voice now a whisper. "When light and shadow cannot coexist, the world suffers."

Selara's hand went to the shard at her neck, its pulse quickening. "And if we restore the Axis?"

The echo hesitated, its form flickering. "Restoring the Axis requires more than uniting the shards. Balance is not a state to be achieved, but a choice to be made—again and again."

Kaelion frowned, his grip on his sword tightening. "What kind of choice?"

The echo's gaze seemed to pierce through him. "The Axis is a reflection of those who wield its power. If you seek to restore it, you must first confront the fractures within yourselves."

The vision shifted again, the barren plain dissolving into darkness. Kaelion found himself alone, the silence pressing in around him like a physical weight. He turned, searching for Selara, but she was nowhere to be seen.

A voice echoed through the void—his own voice, but colder, harsher.

"You think you can redeem yourself? You think one noble act will erase the lives you took?"

Kaelion's chest tightened, his hand instinctively going to the shard at his side. The voice grew louder, the words cutting into him like blades.

"They trusted you. They followed you. And you led them to slaughter."

"No," Kaelion said, his voice trembling. "I didn't—"

The void shifted, and he was back in Solaris, standing in the ruins of a village. The air was thick with the stench of ash and blood, the cries of the dying ringing in his ears. He looked down and saw his hands—stained with blood, his sword slick with crimson.

He staggered back, shaking his head. "This isn't real."

"It is your truth," the echo whispered. "To restore balance, you must first forgive yourself."

Selara stood in her own vision, surrounded by shadows that writhed and twisted like living things. The air was heavy with grief, the scent of burnt wood and scorched earth filling her lungs.

Laryn's voice called to her, faint but unmistakable. "Selara."

Her heart clenched as she turned, her breath catching at the sight of him. He stood just a few paces away, his form wreathed in flickering shadows. His face was etched with pain, but his eyes held the warmth she remembered.

"Laryn," she whispered, tears streaming down her face.

He stepped closer, his hand outstretched. "You can bring me back."

Selara froze, her fingers brushing the shard at her neck. Its pulse quickened, its energy feeding the shadows around her.

"I... I can't," she said, her voice breaking. "You're gone."

"You have the power," Laryn said, his tone insistent. "The shard can undo everything. You can make it right."

Selara's chest heaved with sobs as the shadows coiled tighter around her. The shard's whispers filled her mind, promising her the impossible.

"No," she said, her voice trembling but firm. "You're gone. And I have to let you go."

The shadows recoiled, their grip loosening as Selara's resolve hardened. Laryn's form flickered, his expression softening into a faint smile.

"I'm proud of you," he said, his voice fading into the darkness.

The visions ended as abruptly as they began, and Kaelion and Selara found themselves back in the chamber, their breaths ragged and their bodies trembling.

The echoes had vanished, and the Codex now sat silent on its pedestal, its light dim but steady.

Kaelion turned to Selara, his expression grim. "What did you see?"

She met his gaze, her own eyes filled with a quiet strength. "The truth. And you?"

Kaelion hesitated, then nodded. "The same."

The Codex pulsed faintly, its voice a whisper in their minds.

"The path is revealed. But the journey has just begun."

Chapter Nine: The Gathering Storm

The air outside the Eclipsed Ridge was colder than when they had entered. The perpetual twilight of the Marches hung heavier now, the dim light fractured by low-hanging clouds that churned and swirled like a brewing tempest. Kaelion and Selara emerged from the cavern in silence, their steps slow and deliberate as though each carried an invisible weight.

The Codex had revealed much but answered little. Its voice still echoed faintly in Kaelion's mind, a haunting refrain: "The path is revealed. But the journey has just begun."

Selara was the first to speak.

"What now?" she asked, her tone brittle.

Kaelion tightened the wrappings around his shard, its faint pulse steady beneath the cloth. He gazed at the shifting horizon, where the hills of the Marches seemed to ripple like ocean waves. "We head north. If the Codex is right, the next shard—"

Selara cut him off, her voice sharp. "If the Codex is right? You're putting your faith in a fractured relic that just ripped our minds apart."

Kaelion turned to her, his expression unreadable. "Do you have a better idea?"

Selara opened her mouth to respond but stopped, her gaze shifting to the distance. Her expression darkened, and her hand went instinctively to the shard at her neck. "We're not alone."

Kaelion followed her gaze. On the far edge of the ridge, faint shapes moved against the dusk. At first, they were little more than smudges of darkness, indistinct and blurred. But as they drew closer, their forms became clear—armored figures, their movements precise and unyielding.

"Cyrix's forces," Kaelion muttered, his grip tightening on the hilt of his sword.

Selara's jaw clenched. "How did they find us so quickly?"

Kaelion's eyes narrowed. "They didn't find us. They were waiting."

The first arrow struck the ground near Kaelion's feet, its tip hissing as it buried itself in the soil. A moment later, the ridge erupted into chaos.

The armored soldiers surged forward, their golden armor catching what little light filtered through the twilight sky. At their head was a figure Kaelion recognized immediately—Eryth Kalos, the former commander of Solaris's Radiant Order and Kaelion's mentor turned pursuer.

Kalos's voice carried over the din, cold and commanding. "Kaelion Ashtear! Surrender the shard, and I may yet grant you mercy."

Kaelion's lip curled. "Mercy? That's new for you, Kalos."

The older man sneered. "Your defiance is predictable. And futile." He raised a hand, and the soldiers charged.

Kaelion moved first, his sword flashing as he met the oncoming attackers. The shard at his side pulsed, its energy flowing through him in sharp, rhythmic bursts. Each strike of his blade sent ripples of light through the air, burning through the soldiers' defenses with precision.

Selara stayed close, her shadows weaving around her like a living shield. She lashed out with practiced precision, binding one soldier in tendrils of darkness before shattering his armor with a burst of energy.

"We can't hold them here," she shouted over the clash of steel.

"We don't need to hold them," Kaelion replied, his blade cutting down another soldier. "We need to break through."

The fight was brutal.

Kaelion's movements were fluid and unrelenting, each strike driven by a mix of desperation and determination. The shard's power coursed through him, sharpening his reflexes and lending unnatural strength to his blows.

But the shard took its toll.

His breaths came harder with each swing, his vision blurring at the edges as the shard's energy gnawed at his stamina. He could feel its whispers at the back of his mind, urging him to let go, to give in fully to its power.

Selara fared no better. Her shard flared with each attack, its energy amplifying her shadows but pulling at her emotions, twisting her grief and anger into a volatile storm. Her strikes grew wild, her control slipping as the shard pushed her closer to the edge.

"You're pushing too hard!" Kaelion shouted, parrying a soldier's strike.

"Don't tell me how to fight!" Selara snapped, her shadows lashing out with a ferocity that sent three soldiers sprawling.

Their movements were a chaotic dance of light and shadow, their shards flaring with each strike, each step.

Eryth Kalos watched the battle unfold, his expression cold and calculating. He raised his hand again, signaling a second wave of soldiers. They moved in unison, their golden armor gleaming as they surrounded Kaelion and Selara.

"You cannot win, Kaelion," Kalos said, his voice cutting through the chaos. "The shards will destroy you before I ever have the chance. Surrender now, and I will spare her life."

Kaelion's eyes burned with fury. "You don't get to bargain with her life!"

Kalos smirked, his hand going to the ornate blade at his side. "Then let me end yours."

He moved with the precision of a trained knight, his strikes swift and deadly. Kaelion barely parried the first blow, his arms shaking under the force of Kalos's attack. The older man pressed forward, his strikes relentless, his movements a brutal reminder of the training they had once shared.

"You were my brightest pupil," Kalos said, his voice heavy with disdain. "And my greatest failure."

Kaelion gritted his teeth, his blade clashing against Kalos's with a burst of light. "Maybe you should have taught me better."

Selara struggled against the soldiers surrounding her, her shadows faltering under the sheer number of attackers. The shard at her neck flared brightly, its energy surging through her with reckless abandon. She clenched her fists, forcing the shadows to respond, but her control was slipping.

The soldiers closed in, their weapons gleaming. Selara's breath came in short gasps, her vision narrowing. She felt the shard's whispers growing louder, more insistent.

And then, something shifted.

A burst of energy erupted from her shard, a wave of darkness that surged outward, throwing the soldiers back. Selara staggered, her hands trembling as the shadows writhed around her like living things.

"Selara!" Kaelion shouted, his voice filled with alarm.

She turned to him, her violet eyes glowing faintly. "We have to go. Now."

Kaelion nodded, his sword flashing as he forced Kalos back with a final strike. "Fall back!"

They moved together, their shards pulsing in unison as they fought their way through the remaining soldiers. The air around them crackled with energy, the light of Kaelion's strikes merging with the darkness of Selara's shadows.

At last, they broke free, the path ahead opening into the endless expanse of the Marches.

They didn't stop running until the ridge was a distant blur behind them.

Kaelion collapsed to his knees, his breaths ragged, his sword slipping from his grasp. Selara stood a few paces away, her hand clutching the shard at her neck, her face pale and drawn.

"That was close," Kaelion said, his voice strained.

"Too close," Selara replied.

Kaelion looked at her, his brow furrowing. "What happened back there? That... burst of power?"

Selara hesitated, her fingers brushing the shard. "I don't know. It felt... different. Like the shard was acting on its own."

Kaelion's expression darkened. "That's not a good sign."

"No," Selara agreed. "It's not."

They sat in silence, the weight of their exhaustion pressing down on them. The shards pulsed faintly, their rhythm steady but unyielding.

"We can't keep running forever," Kaelion said.

Selara nodded, her gaze fixed on the horizon. "Then we'd better find a way to stop them before they stop us."

The storm was coming, and the shadows were closing in.

Chapter Ten: Threads of Discord

The air in the makeshift camp was heavy with tension. The fire crackled weakly, its embers glowing faintly against the muted hues of the Marches. Kaelion and Selara sat on opposite sides of the flames, their exhaustion palpable. Shadows flickered across their faces, creating the illusion of fractures—a reflection of the unseen rifts growing between them.

Selara stared into the fire, her hand absently brushing the shard at her neck. Its pulse had grown erratic since the battle at the ridge, the rhythm matching the turmoil in her mind. She hadn't spoken since they had stopped to rest, and the silence stretched between them like a taut rope.

Kaelion finally broke it.

"What happened back there?" he asked, his voice low but insistent. "That power—was it you, or the shard?"

Selara's jaw tightened. "Does it matter?"

Kaelion leaned forward, his gaze hard. "It matters if the shard is starting to take over."

She glared at him, her eyes narrowing. "And what about your shard? You think it's not whispering to you? I see the way you wield it, like it's the only thing keeping you alive."

Kaelion's grip on his sword tightened. "We don't have a choice. The shards are the only reason we're still standing."

"And they're the same reason we're falling apart," Selara shot back. Her voice trembled, the edges of her composure fraying. "These things—they don't just amplify our power. They amplify everything. Every fear, every doubt, every—"

She stopped abruptly, her hand clenching into a fist.

"Every loss," Kaelion finished quietly.

Selara's breath hitched, and for a moment, her anger gave way to something raw, something vulnerable. She looked away, her shoulders tense.

"We don't have time for this," she said, her voice barely above a whisper.

Kaelion didn't push further. He leaned back, his gaze drifting to the dark expanse beyond the firelight. The shadows of the Marches seemed deeper now, more oppressive, as if the land itself was closing in on them.

The silence was broken by the sound of footsteps—soft but deliberate.

Kaelion's hand went to his sword as he rose to his feet, his eyes scanning the darkness. Selara followed suit, her shadows coiling around her hands like smoke.

From the edge of the firelight, a figure emerged. He was cloaked in the twilight hues of the Marches, his form blending seamlessly with the surrounding dusk. His face was partially obscured by a hood, but his eyes gleamed with an unsettling brightness.

"Who are you?" Kaelion demanded, his sword raised.

The figure stopped just short of the firelight, his movements calm and measured. "A traveler," he said, his voice smooth and even. "Much like yourselves."

Selara narrowed her eyes. "Travelers don't usually sneak up on camps in the middle of the night."

The man chuckled softly. "Perhaps not. But the paths of the Marches are rarely traveled without purpose."

Kaelion stepped forward, his sword glinting faintly in the firelight. "State yours, then. What do you want?"

The man's gaze shifted to the shards, his expression unreadable. "To warn you."

Selara tensed. "Warn us about what?"

"About the storm you're chasing," the man said. His voice was laced with an edge of knowing, as if he had seen something they had not. "The shards are not tools to be wielded. They are seeds of destruction, planted long ago. And you, shard-bearers, are their harvest."

Kaelion's grip on his sword tightened. "What are you talking about?"

The man stepped closer, his face now partially illuminated. He was older than Kaelion had first thought, his features lined with age and weariness. "The Codex. The Axis. You think you can restore balance by reuniting what was broken. But you fail to see the truth."

Selara's voice was sharp. "And what truth is that?"

The man's eyes met hers, their intensity unwavering. "That the Axis didn't shatter on its own. It was broken deliberately."

The words hung in the air like a thunderclap, their weight settling heavily on Kaelion and Selara.

Kaelion's brow furrowed. "Deliberately? By who?"

The man's gaze darkened. "By those who thought they could control it. Those who believed they could harness its power without consequence. But they failed, as you will fail if you continue down this path."

Selara stepped forward, her shadows flickering with her rising anger. "If you know so much, then tell us what we're supposed to do. Sit back and let the world fall apart?"

The man didn't flinch. "The world has already fallen apart. The shards are not a solution—they are a curse. And the more you use them, the more they will twist you."

Kaelion's jaw tightened, his mind racing. The shard at his side pulsed faintly, as if in response to the man's words. He glanced at Selara, her expression a mixture of defiance and doubt, and felt the same turmoil stirring within himself.

"What's your name?" Kaelion asked.

The man hesitated for a moment before answering. "Tavriel," he said. "And I was once a shard-bearer, like you."

Tavriel stepped fully into the firelight, his presence commanding despite his unassuming frame. He reached into the folds of his cloak and produced a shard—not radiant like Kaelion's or shadowed like Selara's, but faintly translucent, its edges glinting like fractured glass.

"This," Tavriel said, holding the shard aloft, "is all that remains of what I carried. I cast aside its power long ago, but its whispers never truly leave."

Selara studied him carefully, her suspicion tempered by curiosity. "If you gave up your shard, why are you here? Why warn us now?"

"Because the storm you chase will not spare you," Tavriel said. "And because the Codex has begun to stir. Its voice calls to those who would claim the Axis—not to restore it, but to control it."

Kaelion's thoughts turned to Cyrix, the memory of their confrontation still fresh in his mind. "You're talking about Cyrix."

Tavriel nodded. "He is one of many. The shards amplify not only power but ambition. They call to those who crave control, who seek to bend the world to their will. Cyrix is only the beginning."

The fire crackled softly, its light casting flickering shadows on the trio.

Kaelion's voice broke the silence. "If we're not supposed to restore the Axis, then what are we supposed to do?"

Tavriel's gaze was steady. "You must find a new path. The Codex has revealed itself to you, and it will guide you if you let it. But you must first understand the truth of the shards and the cost of balance."

Selara's voice was sharp. "And how do we do that?"

Tavriel stepped closer, his eyes gleaming with a quiet intensity. "By walking the edge of light and shadow. By embracing both, not as opposites, but as parts of a whole."

His words sent a chill through Kaelion, the weight of their meaning sinking in. The shards pulsed faintly, their rhythm a discordant counterpoint to the quiet of the Marches.

"We leave at dawn," Kaelion said finally, his voice firm. "If the Codex is guiding us, then we follow it. Whatever the cost."

Selara glanced at him, her expression unreadable, but she nodded.

Tavriel smiled faintly, his expression tinged with sorrow. "Then may the path show you what you need, not what you want."

The fire flickered, and the shadows deepened.

Chapter Eleven: Beneath the Dusk Veil

The Twilight Marches stretched before them, vast and unknowable. Kaelion, Selara, and Tavriel moved with purpose, their steps muted against the silken grass that shimmered faintly beneath the eternal dusk. The shards at Kaelion and Selara's sides pulsed with their steady rhythm, but their hum felt quieter here, as though the Marches themselves dampened their restless energy.

Kaelion kept his hand close to his sword, his gaze sweeping the horizon. The presence of Tavriel unsettled him. The man walked with an ease that belied his warnings from the previous night, his movements fluid and deliberate, as though he already knew the path ahead.

Selara walked a few paces ahead, her shoulders tense, her silence sharper than her usual barbs. She hadn't spoken since they had left the camp, and the weight of her unspoken thoughts hung heavily between them.

Tavriel finally broke the silence.

"The Marches are more than a passage," he said, his voice low but clear. "They are a crucible. A place where those who tread their paths are tested, reshaped."

Kaelion frowned. "Tested how?"

Tavriel's gaze turned distant. "The Marches reveal what lies beneath the surface. Your fears, your desires, your truths. They force you to confront the parts of yourself you'd rather leave buried."

Selara snorted softly. "Sounds like another way of saying we're going to get lost in our own heads."

Tavriel smiled faintly. "Not lost. Found."

Kaelion didn't like the sound of it, but he said nothing. The path ahead was growing narrower, the hills rising into jagged peaks veined with faint streaks of silver. The air felt different here, heavier, as if it carried the weight of countless stories whispered into the twilight.

As they climbed, the landscape shifted. The hills gave way to rocky outcroppings, their surfaces carved with patterns that seemed to shimmer and move when viewed from the corner of the eye.

Kaelion paused at one of the carvings, his brow furrowing. "What is this?"

Tavriel stepped beside him, his fingers brushing the stone. "Marks left by those who walked this path before us. Some say they are warnings. Others say they are memories, etched into the land itself."

Selara's voice was laced with skepticism. "Memories of what?"

"Of the shards," Tavriel said. "Of the Axis. Of those who sought to restore it and failed."

Kaelion felt a chill run down his spine. He turned away from the carvings, his hand tightening on his sword. "Then let's make sure we're not adding our story to these stones."

They continued in silence, the path growing steeper. The air grew colder, carrying a faint metallic tang that made Kaelion's shard pulse erratically. He glanced at Selara, whose own shard was glowing faintly, its energy threading into the shadows around her.

"Do you feel that?" he asked.

She nodded, her expression grim. "Something's close."

Tavriel stopped suddenly, his head tilting as if listening to a distant sound. "We're nearing the Veil," he said.

"The Veil?" Kaelion asked.

"The threshold between the Marches and the Eclipsed Ridge," Tavriel replied. "It's a place where light and shadow converge. Few have passed through unscathed."

Selara raised an eyebrow. "And you thought now was a good time to mention that?"

Tavriel's faint smile returned. "Would it have stopped you?"

Kaelion didn't answer. He turned his focus to the path ahead, his sword drawn and ready.

The Veil came into view gradually, its presence more felt than seen. The air shimmered with an unnatural light, threads of gold and black weaving together in a chaotic dance. The ground beneath their feet grew uneven, the grass giving way to a surface that felt brittle and unstable.

Kaelion stepped cautiously, his eyes scanning the horizon. "What are we looking for?"

"The Veil is alive," Tavriel said. "It will show you what it wants you to see."

Before Kaelion could ask what that meant, the ground beneath him shifted, and the world around him dissolved.

Kaelion found himself standing in the ruins of a battlefield. The sky was dark, streaked with ash and fire, and the air was thick with the stench of blood. Broken bodies lay scattered across the ground, their armor bearing the unmistakable insignia of Solaris.

His heart clenched as he recognized the scene. It was the village. The place where everything had gone wrong.

He heard the screams before he saw the survivors—civilians huddled together, their faces etched with terror. They looked at him, their eyes filled with accusations.

"Why didn't you save us?" a voice called out.

Kaelion turned to see a boy, no older than ten, standing among the bodies. His face was pale, his eyes hollow.

"I tried," Kaelion said, his voice trembling.

"You didn't try hard enough," the boy replied.

Kaelion staggered back, the weight of the shard at his side growing heavier. The boy stepped closer, his voice rising.

"You could have stopped it. You could have saved us. But you didn't."

Selara found herself in her studio, the familiar scent of stone dust and shadow magic filling the air. Her hands worked on a sculpture, the form of a figure emerging from the onyx—Laryn, his face as perfect as she remembered.

"Selara," his voice whispered, soft and warm.

She froze, her hands trembling. "Laryn?"

The figure stepped from the sculpture, its movements fluid and graceful. His eyes met hers, filled with the same love and warmth she had carried in her heart for so long.

"You can bring me back," he said, his voice soft but insistent.

Selara's chest tightened. "I can't."

"Yes, you can," Laryn replied, stepping closer. "The shard—its power is yours. Use it. Bring me back, Selara."

The shard at her neck flared, its energy surging through her veins. The shadows around her grew darker, more insistent, as if feeding on her doubt.

"I... I don't know," she whispered.

Tavriel stood at the edge of the Veil, his form wavering as the visions played out around him. His shard glowed faintly, its energy a quiet pulse in the chaos.

"They will find their truth," he murmured to himself. "Or they will fall."

The Veil pulsed, its threads of light and shadow weaving tighter, binding the travelers to their trials.

Kaelion dropped to his knees, the boy's voice echoing in his mind. The shard at his side pulsed violently, its whispers clawing at his thoughts.

"No," he said, his voice breaking. "This isn't real."

"It's as real as your failure," the boy said, his form shifting into a towering figure wreathed in shadow. "And it will be your undoing."

Kaelion gritted his teeth, his hand gripping the shard. "Not this time."

The light of the shard flared, and the battlefield dissolved into nothingness.

Selara clenched her fists, the shadows writhing around her as Laryn's form loomed over her.

"You're not him," she said, her voice steady despite the tears streaming down her face.

The figure paused, its form flickering.

"You're not him!" she screamed, her shard's energy surging outward. The studio shattered, and the shadows receded, leaving her alone once more.

Kaelion and Selara emerged from their visions at the same time, their breaths ragged, their bodies trembling. Tavriel watched them, his expression solemn.

"You passed the first trial," he said.

Kaelion looked at him, his jaw tightening. "How many more are there?"

Tavriel's smile was faint but knowing. "As many as it takes."

The Veil shimmered behind them, its threads of light and shadow weaving anew.

Chapter Twelve: The Twisting Path

The Veil settled behind them like a door closing softly, its presence fading into the dusk. Kaelion, Selara, and Tavriel stood at the edge of a new terrain—a stark contrast to the gentle hills of the Twilight Marches. The land ahead was rugged and jagged, the ground split into deep fissures that emitted faint trails of vapor, as though the earth itself was exhaling.

The sky above them seemed darker here, the perpetual twilight thickened into a deep indigo that blurred the line between horizon and void. Stars glittered faintly, too distant to offer guidance. The only light came from the shards, their soft glow a steady rhythm that pulsed in harmony with the quiet hum of the landscape.

Selara exhaled sharply, her breath visible in the chilled air. "This place feels wrong."

"It is wrong," Tavriel replied. His voice was calm, though his gaze was heavy with memory. "This is the Twisting Path. A scar left by the Axis's fracture. It leads to the heart of the Ridge, but it is not a path meant for the unprepared."

Kaelion tightened the strap of his sword sheath, his eyes scanning the fractured ground. "We've come this far. We're not turning back now."

"Then tread carefully," Tavriel warned. "This place does not simply test your mind. It bends reality to reflect your flaws, your doubts, your weaknesses. If you stray too far from your resolve, you will lose yourself entirely."

Selara shot him a sharp look. "Would have been nice to know that before we crossed the Veil."

Tavriel's faint smile returned. "Would you have listened?"

Selara opened her mouth to retort but stopped herself. Instead, she tightened her cloak around her shoulders and stepped forward, her shadows swirling faintly at her heels.

The path wound through jagged outcroppings of stone, the air growing colder with every step. Kaelion took the lead, his sword drawn, its blade glinting faintly in the dim light. Selara followed close behind, her shard glowing softly at her neck. Tavriel brought up the rear, his presence steady but distant, as though he were walking through a memory rather than alongside them.

The hum of the shards grew louder as they moved deeper into the Ridge. It wasn't the chaotic pulse Kaelion had grown used to—it was slower, more deliberate, as though the shards were responding to something buried within the land itself.

"This place is alive," Kaelion muttered, his voice barely audible over the wind.

Selara glanced at him, her expression tight. "Alive? More like cursed."

"The two are not mutually exclusive," Tavriel said.

As if in answer, the ground beneath their feet shifted, a faint tremor running through the stone. The air around them grew heavier, pressing against their senses like an unseen weight.

Kaelion froze, his hand tightening on his sword. "Did you feel that?"

Selara nodded, her shadows flickering uneasily. "Something's watching us."

The first attack came without warning.

A rift opened in the ground ahead, spilling forth a wave of energy that crackled with light and shadow. From within the rift emerged a creature—a monstrous amalgamation of jagged stone and flickering energy. Its form was unstable, its limbs shifting between solid and ethereal, its eyes glowing with a malevolent light.

Kaelion moved on instinct. His sword arced through the air, striking the creature's arm and sending a burst of light through its form. The creature howled, its voice a discordant wail that sent shivers down his spine.

Selara reacted just as quickly. Her shadows surged forward, wrapping around the creature's legs and holding it in place. The shard at her neck flared, amplifying her control, but she gritted her teeth as the creature fought against her grip.

"This thing isn't natural," she shouted.

"It's not meant to be," Tavriel said, his voice steady as he stepped forward. "The Twisting Path creates what it needs to test you. This creature is a manifestation of your doubts—your fears given form."

Kaelion growled as he drove his blade into the creature's chest, the shard at his side pulsing with raw energy. "Then let's end it."

The creature dissolved with a final, piercing wail, its form breaking apart into motes of light and shadow that faded into the air. The rift closed with a low rumble, leaving the path silent once more.

They pressed on, the tension between them growing heavier with each step. The Twisting Path seemed to shift and change as they walked, the terrain twisting into impossible shapes that defied logic.

At one point, they came to a bridge of stone suspended over a chasm that stretched endlessly into the void. The bridge was narrow, its surface slick with frost, and the wind howled through the gap with a mournful cry.

Kaelion went first, his movements slow and deliberate. The shard at his side pulsed with each step, its energy steadying his balance even as the wind threatened to pull him off course.

Selara followed, her shadows clinging to the edges of the bridge like anchors. She moved with practiced precision, her focus unwavering despite the growing hum of her shard.

Tavriel crossed last, his steps sure and unhurried. He paused at the center of the bridge, his gaze turning upward to the darkened sky.

"What are you looking at?" Kaelion called from the other side.

Tavriel didn't answer immediately. When he did, his voice was distant. "The sky remembers. Even in a place like this, it carries the memory of what came before."

Kaelion frowned, his unease deepening. He turned his attention back to the path ahead, unwilling to linger on Tavriel's cryptic words.

The final stretch of the Twisting Path brought them to a narrow canyon, its walls carved with the same shifting patterns they had seen before. The air here was thick with energy, the hum of the shards resonating with an almost physical force.

Selara stopped suddenly, her hand going to the shard at her neck. "Do you hear that?"

Kaelion listened, his brow furrowing. There was a sound beneath the hum of the shards—a low, rhythmic thrum that seemed to echo from deep within the canyon.

Tavriel's expression darkened. "The Axis's resonance. We're close."

"Close to what?" Selara asked.

"To the place where light and shadow meet," Tavriel said. "The heart of the Ridge. The shards will reveal their purpose there—but only if you survive the final trial."

Kaelion's grip on his sword tightened. The Twisting Path had tested their resolve, their strength, their very sense of self. Whatever awaited them at the heart of the Ridge would demand more than all of that combined.

"Let's finish this," he said, his voice steady despite the weight in his chest.

Selara nodded, her gaze hard. "Let's."

Together, they stepped into the canyon, the light of the shards illuminating the way forward.

Chapter Thirteen: Whispers in the Canyon

The canyon walls loomed on either side, their surfaces carved with ever-shifting patterns of light and shadow. Kaelion, Selara, and Tavriel moved cautiously, their footsteps echoing faintly against the stone. The air was colder here, the faint metallic tang from earlier now sharp enough to sting the back of their throats.

The hum of the shards had grown louder, their resonance vibrating in Kaelion's chest like a second heartbeat. Each step seemed to draw them deeper into something vast and unknowable, the edges of their reality bending under the weight of unseen forces.

Selara was the first to speak, her voice low and strained. "This place feels... alive."

"It is alive," Tavriel said, his tone solemn. "The heart of the Ridge is a nexus of the Axis's energy. What you feel is its pulse—what remains of it, anyway."

Kaelion scanned the canyon walls, his sword drawn. "And the shards? They're connected to this, aren't they?"

Tavriel nodded. "The shards resonate with the Axis's memory. The closer we come to its core, the more they will reveal—but only to those who can withstand its truth."

Selara shot him a sharp look. "And if we can't?"

"Then this canyon will be your tomb," Tavriel said simply.

The path narrowed, forcing them to walk single file. The air grew heavier, pressing against their senses like a physical weight. Faint whispers began to echo through the canyon, their source indiscernible.

Kaelion froze, his grip tightening on his sword. "Did you hear that?"

Selara nodded, her shadows flickering uneasily around her. "Whispers. But from where?"

"They come from the Axis," Tavriel said, his voice barely above a whisper. "Or rather, from what it remembers."

Kaelion's brow furrowed. "The Axis remembers?"

"It remembers everything," Tavriel said. "Every choice, every failure, every fracture. The shards carry fragments of its memory, and here, at the heart of the Ridge, those memories come alive."

As if on cue, the whispers grew louder, their voices overlapping in a chaotic symphony. Kaelion couldn't make out the words, but the tone was unmistakable—pleading, warning, accusing.

The canyon opened into a wide clearing, its center dominated by a massive, circular platform of stone. The platform's surface was etched with the same shifting patterns as the canyon walls, but these were larger, more intricate, their shapes twisting and spiraling like the shards' resonance marks.

At the center of the platform stood a pedestal, its surface glowing faintly with a pulsating light.

"The Codex guided us here," Tavriel said, his gaze fixed on the pedestal. "This is the Axis's voice, its memory made manifest."

Kaelion approached cautiously, his shard flaring with each step. "And what happens when we reach it?"

"You listen," Tavriel said.

Kaelion exchanged a glance with Selara, who looked just as wary as he felt. But there was no turning back now. They stepped onto the platform together, the stone beneath their feet humming with energy.

The pedestal's glow intensified as they approached, its light spilling across the clearing. The whispers grew louder, their voices blending into a single, resonant tone that filled the air.

Selara's breath hitched. "It's... speaking to us."

Kaelion's jaw tightened. "What's it saying?"

Tavriel stepped forward, his expression solemn. "Not saying. Showing."

The light of the pedestal flared, and the world around them dissolved.

Kaelion found himself standing in a vast, featureless void, the ground beneath him smooth and reflective like a mirror. The air was still, the silence oppressive. Across the void, he saw Selara and Tavriel, their forms faintly distorted by the reflective surface.

A voice echoed through the void, soft and melodic. "Shard-bearers. Why do you seek balance?"

Kaelion hesitated, his thoughts racing. The shard at his side pulsed faintly, as though urging him to speak.

"To fix what was broken," he said finally. "To stop this world from tearing itself apart."

The voice seemed to shift, its tone growing colder. "And what will you sacrifice to achieve this balance?"

Kaelion's breath caught. The question struck something deep within him, a place he wasn't ready to confront.

Selara stood rigid, the voice reverberating in her mind. The void around her began to shift, shadows coalescing into familiar shapes. She saw Laryn's face, his expression soft and kind, his hand outstretched toward her.

"Selara," the voice whispered, layered with his. "What will you give to bring balance? Will you sacrifice your pain, your grief, your anger?"

Her chest tightened, the shard at her neck pulsing erratically. "I can't let it go," she said, her voice trembling. "It's all I have left."

The shadows around her darkened, their forms pressing closer. "Then you are not ready," the voice said.

"No!" Selara shouted, her voice ringing through the void. "I won't let you decide that!"

The shadows recoiled slightly, their edges flickering, but the voice remained silent.

Tavriel stood apart, his form steady despite the chaos around him. His shard glowed faintly, its pulse in perfect sync with the voice.

"You already know my answer," he said quietly.

The void rippled, and the voice softened. "Yes. You have already paid the price."

Tavriel closed his eyes, his expression tinged with sorrow. "And yet the cost remains."

Kaelion's reflection shifted, the mirrored surface beneath him revealing scenes from his past. He saw the village—the one he had failed to save. He saw the faces of those he had led, their expressions twisted in pain and betrayal.

"You seek redemption," the voice said. "But redemption is not earned through power. It is earned through surrender."

Kaelion shook his head, his fists clenched. "I can't surrender. If I do, people will die."

"People will die regardless," the voice replied. "The question is whether their lives will mean something."

The shard at his side flared, its energy surging through him. Kaelion fell to his knees, his breath ragged.

The void began to fracture, the reflective surface splitting into shards of light and shadow. The voice grew louder, its tone commanding.

"The path forward demands more than strength. It demands truth. Surrender your fear. Surrender your grief. Only then will the Axis be whole again."

Kaelion looked up, his gaze meeting Selara's. She stood across the void, her shadows flickering around her, her expression a mix of defiance and pain.

They didn't need to speak. The weight of the moment pressed down on them both, the truth of the voice cutting through their doubts.

Together, they reached for their shards, their hands trembling as the void collapsed around them.

The clearing returned, the pedestal's light fading into a faint, steady glow. Kaelion and Selara staggered back, their breaths ragged, their bodies trembling. Tavriel stood beside them, his expression calm but somber.

"The Axis has spoken," he said quietly. "The question now is whether you can bear its answer."

Kaelion glanced at Selara, her face pale but determined. He felt the weight of his shard pressing against his side, its pulse slower now, more deliberate.

"We'll see," Kaelion said, his voice steady despite the uncertainty in his chest.

The path forward stretched into the unknown, and the storm gathered on the horizon.

Chapter Fourteen: Fractured Promises

The storm in the distance loomed ever closer, its swirling clouds of violet and black a harbinger of the chaos to come. Kaelion, Selara, and Tavriel stood at the edge of the canyon, their breaths visible in the chill air. The faint glow of the shards reflected in their eyes, casting their faces in shifting hues of light and shadow.

The tension between them was palpable, thickening the air with unspoken fears and doubts. Kaelion was the first to break the silence.

"The Axis gave us answers," he said, his voice low but firm. "But it also gave us a choice."

Selara crossed her arms, her eyes narrowing. "And what happens if we choose wrong? It didn't exactly come with instructions, Kaelion."

Kaelion turned to face her, his expression tight. "We don't have the luxury of second-guessing. If we don't act, Cyrix will force his version of the Eclipse on the world—and everyone will pay the price."

"And if we act without understanding what we're doing?" Selara countered, her voice sharp. "You heard what the Axis said. Balance isn't just about power. It's about what we're willing to give up. What if we're not ready to make that sacrifice?"

Kaelion's jaw tightened, his hand brushing the shard at his side. "Then we'll make ourselves ready."

Tavriel watched them silently, his expression unreadable. When he finally spoke, his voice was calm but edged with a quiet urgency.

"The Axis revealed its truth to you," he said. "But truth is not the same as understanding. If you act out of fear or anger, you will only fracture it further."

Kaelion turned to him, his eyes narrowing. "Then guide us. You've seen more than we have. You've walked this path before. What do we do?"

Tavriel's gaze shifted to the horizon, where the storm churned with an almost sentient fury. "The Axis demands balance. To restore it, you must surrender the parts of yourselves that tip the scales. Your fears, your grief, your guilt. Only then can the shards unite without consuming you."

Selara shook her head, her voice trembling with anger. "You make it sound so simple. Just 'let go,' and everything will fall into place. But how do you let go of something that's defined you? How do you give up the one thing that keeps you moving forward?"

Tavriel met her gaze, his expression softening. "By choosing something greater than yourself."

The ground beneath their feet trembled faintly, the resonance of the shards growing stronger. The storm on the horizon pulsed in response, its edges flickering with bursts of light and shadow.

Kaelion glanced at Selara, her defiance mirrored in his own. He didn't have an answer for her—didn't know if there even was one. All he knew was that every step they took brought them closer to a confrontation they couldn't avoid.

"We need to keep moving," he said, his voice quiet but firm. "The Codex showed us the way. We follow it until the end."

Selara didn't respond immediately. Her eyes lingered on the shard at her neck, its pulse matching the rhythm of her heart. Finally, she nodded, though her expression remained guarded.

Tavriel gestured to the jagged path ahead, his voice steady. "The storm will lead you to the Axis's core. But it will also draw Cyrix to the same place. He will not wait for you to make your choice."

The journey toward the storm was grueling. The path twisted and turned, the air growing colder and thinner with each step. The shards pulsed steadily, their hum resonating in the stone beneath their feet.

Kaelion led the way, his sword drawn, its blade glinting faintly in the dim light. The memories of the Axis's vision lingered in his mind, the weight of its truth pressing against his thoughts like a vice.

Behind him, Selara moved in silence, her shadows flickering around her like restless spirits. Her thoughts were a whirlwind of doubt and anger, the shard at her neck a constant reminder of the choice she didn't know how to make.

Tavriel followed at a distance, his steps unhurried, his gaze distant. He carried himself with the air of someone who had already seen the ending—and wasn't certain whether he liked it.

They stopped at the edge of a narrow ridge, the storm now a towering wall of chaos just beyond their reach. Lightning crackled within its depths, illuminating the swirling clouds with bursts of violet and gold.

Selara's voice cut through the silence. "This is it, isn't it? The core of the Axis."

Tavriel nodded. "The place where light and shadow first collided. Where the Axis fractured, and the shards were born."

Kaelion tightened his grip on his sword. "And where we'll finish this."

A sound behind them made him turn sharply. He raised his blade, his eyes scanning the path they had just traveled.

"We're not alone," he said.

From the shadows of the ridge, figures emerged—dozens of them, their armor glinting faintly in the storm's light. At their head was a figure Kaelion knew all too well: Lord Cyrix, his cloak billowing behind him like the wings of a predator.

Cyrix's voice carried over the wind, cold and commanding. "You've come far, shard-bearers. But this is where your journey ends."

Kaelion stepped forward, his blade raised. "You won't stop us, Cyrix."

Cyrix chuckled, the sound low and menacing. "Stop you? I've been guiding you. Every step you've taken has brought you closer to me—and closer to the truth."

Selara's eyes narrowed. "What truth?"

"The truth of the Eclipse," Cyrix said, his voice reverent. "The shards are not tools for restoring balance. They are keys to unlocking a new world—a world where light and shadow are not at war, but united under my control."

Kaelion's grip on his sword tightened. "You think you can control the shards? You can barely control yourself."

Cyrix's gaze hardened. "You mistake my resolve for weakness. I have seen the Axis's core. I have seen what it can become. And I will wield its power to remake this world in my image."

The storm surged behind Cyrix, its energy crackling with renewed intensity. The shards at Kaelion and Selara's sides pulsed violently, their resonance clashing with the storm's rhythm.

Selara stepped forward, her shadows coiling around her like living things. "You're insane if you think we'll let you do that."

Cyrix smiled faintly. "And you're naive if you think you can stop me."

He raised his hand, and the storm erupted into chaos. Lightning streaked across the sky, and the ground beneath them shook violently. The ridge began to crumble, the path ahead splitting into jagged fragments.

Kaelion glanced at Selara, his expression grim. "We have to get to the core before he does."

She nodded, her shadows surging forward to stabilize the crumbling path. "Then let's move."

Chapter Fifteen: Into the Storm

The storm loomed over them like a living entity, its swirling mass of violet and gold crackling with chaotic energy. Every breath felt charged, the air saturated with an unnatural hum that resonated in Kaelion's chest, vibrating in time with the shard at his side.

Selara's shadows lashed out against the winds, weaving a protective cocoon around her as she forged ahead. Her shard burned against her skin, its pulse erratic, like a second heartbeat fighting to dominate her own.

Behind them, Cyrix's forces moved with purpose, their golden armor glinting with an eerie light. The sound of their boots striking the fractured stone was almost rhythmic, a grim march toward their shared destination. At their head, Cyrix walked with unsettling calm, his cloak billowing in the storm's gale.

"We don't have much time," Kaelion said, his voice nearly lost in the howling wind.

Selara didn't look back. "Then stop talking and move!"

The path narrowed as they ascended, the fractured ridge crumbling beneath their feet. Lightning arced across the sky, illuminating the storm's depth and revealing glimpses of something massive at its center—a pulsing orb of light and shadow, suspended within a vortex of energy.

"The Axis's core," Tavriel said, his voice steady despite the chaos around them. "It's close."

Kaelion glanced over his shoulder. Cyrix and his forces were gaining ground, their movements relentless. He turned back to Selara, his expression hardening. "We need to split up. If we both go for the core, we'll make it too easy for him to pin us down."

Selara hesitated, her shadows flickering with uncertainty. "You're suggesting we divide our strength?"

"I'm suggesting we divide his attention," Kaelion said. "You take the higher path. I'll go straight for the core. Tavriel—"

"I'll hold the ridge," Tavriel interrupted, his tone resolute. "You'll need someone to slow him down."

Selara frowned, her gaze flicking between the two men. "This is reckless."

Kaelion nodded. "It is. But it's the only chance we've got."

They moved without further argument, their paths diverging as the ridge split into two jagged trails. Kaelion descended toward the core, his sword drawn, its blade glowing faintly in the storm's light. The shard at his side pulsed stronger now, its energy surging through him with each step.

The wind howled around him, carrying whispers that sounded both familiar and alien. They clawed at his mind, dredging up memories of failure and doubt, but he pressed on, his grip on his sword tightening.

Ahead, the core pulsed with an almost hypnotic rhythm, its light casting long shadows that seemed to writhe like living things.

Selara's path was treacherous, the higher trail exposed to the full force of the storm. Her shadows coiled around her feet, anchoring her to the crumbling stone as she climbed.

The shard at her neck burned hotter now, its whispers growing louder, more insistent. It promised her strength, control, the power to shape the world as she saw fit.

"You could stop him," it seemed to say. "You could end this—all of this—with a single choice."

Selara gritted her teeth, forcing the whispers aside. "Not like that," she muttered. "Never like that."

Lightning flashed, and for a moment, she saw Cyrix below, his forces spreading out across the ridge. He moved with purpose, his shard glowing with a dark, almost malevolent light.

Selara's shadows surged forward, reaching for him, but he glanced up as if sensing her presence. His smile was faint but filled with certainty, and he raised his hand, summoning a burst of energy that shattered her attack.

"Soon," his voice carried over the storm, taunting and confident.

Selara snarled, her shadows snapping back to her as she pressed forward.

Tavriel stood at the center of the ridge, his cloak whipping in the wind as Cyrix's forces approached. His shard pulsed faintly, its energy steady but restrained.

One of the soldiers charged, his blade gleaming with captured light. Tavriel stepped aside with a fluid motion, his hand brushing the soldier's armor. The shard's energy surged through him, and the soldier froze mid-strike, his weapon clattering to the ground.

Tavriel's voice was quiet but firm. "You do not belong here."

The soldier fell, his body collapsing into shadow and light that dissolved into the storm.

Cyrix slowed his approach, his eyes narrowing as he studied Tavriel. "You again. The seer who hides in riddles and half-truths."

Tavriel's expression didn't change. "I speak only the truths you refuse to see, Cyrix."

Cyrix's shard flared, its energy surging around him like a second skin. "And yet here you stand, a relic of the past, guarding what you can never reclaim."

Tavriel's gaze didn't waver. "I guard what I can because I know what it means to lose everything."

Kaelion reached the core, its light and shadow swirling together in an intricate dance. The energy was overwhelming, pressing against him like a physical force. The shard at his side flared brightly, resonating with the core's pulse.

He stepped closer, his breath coming in short gasps. The whispers grew louder, their voices blending into a single, commanding tone.

"Shard-bearer. You stand at the precipice. What will you choose?"

Kaelion gritted his teeth. "I'll choose balance. I'll choose to fix what was broken."

The core pulsed violently, its energy surging outward in a wave that knocked him to his knees.

"Balance demands sacrifice. Are you prepared to surrender yourself?"

Selara reached the higher vantage point, her shadows stretching out toward the core. She could feel its pull, its power resonating with her shard. The storm raged around her, but her focus was unshaken.

Below, she saw Kaelion kneeling before the core, his form illuminated by its light. And she saw Cyrix closing in, his forces surging toward the final confrontation.

Her shadows coiled tightly around her, their energy thrumming with urgency. The shard at her neck whispered its promise again, louder this time.

"You can stop him," it urged. "You can protect him. All you have to do is let me in."

Selara's hand clenched into a fist. The storm roared, and the shadows surged forward.

Chapter Sixteen: Collision at the Core

Kaelion forced himself to his feet, the energy of the Axis's core pressing against him like a wall of fire and ice. The shard at his side pulsed violently, in perfect rhythm with the swirling mass of light and shadow before him. Every breath burned in his lungs, and every step toward the core felt like a battle against the weight of his own fears.

Behind him, the sounds of battle echoed through the storm. Cyrix's forces clashed with Tavriel's illusions and Selara's shadows, their cries lost to the howling winds. Kaelion didn't dare look back. The core demanded his attention, its presence a beacon that drowned out everything else.

As he reached the edge of the platform where the core hovered, he saw it clearly for the first time—a massive, spinning sphere of energy, its surface rippling with patterns that mirrored those on the shards. It felt alive, pulsing with a resonance that vibrated through the very air.

A voice, ancient and resonant, filled the space. "You stand before the heart of what was and what could be. Speak, shard-bearer. Why do you seek balance?"

Kaelion hesitated, his grip tightening on his sword. "Because the world needs it. Because without it, we'll destroy ourselves."

The voice seemed to shift, its tone deepening. "And what are you willing to surrender to achieve it?"

The platform shook as Cyrix stepped onto it, his shard glowing with a fierce, unnatural light. His presence felt oppressive, his energy clashing violently with the core's resonance.

"You don't belong here," Kaelion said, turning to face him.

Cyrix smirked, his cloak billowing in the storm's gale. "You still think this is about belonging? This is about power, Kaelion. About the strength to shape the world as it should be."

Kaelion raised his sword, its blade gleaming faintly in the light of the core. "The world doesn't need shaping. It needs saving."

Cyrix laughed, the sound cold and hollow. "And you think you can save it by clinging to the old ways? The Axis doesn't need balance. It needs control—my control."

Cyrix raised his hand, and his shard flared, sending a wave of energy surging toward Kaelion. Kaelion moved instinctively, his sword slicing through the air, the shard at his side amplifying his movements. The clash of light and shadow sent a shockwave rippling through the platform, the core flickering in response.

Above them, Selara watched the battle unfold, her shadows curling tightly around her. The shard at her neck burned hotter than ever, its whispers growing louder, more insistent.

"You can end this," it urged. "You have the power. Use it."

Selara clenched her fists, her breath coming in short, sharp bursts. Below, Kaelion and Cyrix's battle raged, their energy colliding in bursts of light and shadow. The core pulsed violently, its resonance throwing the storm into chaos.

She felt the shard's power surging through her, tempting her with its promise of control. All she had to do was let go—let it take over, let it guide her.

But something inside her resisted.

"No," she whispered, her voice trembling. "I won't let it control me."

The shard's whispers grew harsher, more demanding. "Then you will fail. You will lose him. And everything will fall apart."

Kaelion staggered back, his sword barely deflecting another wave of Cyrix's energy. The older man's movements were relentless, his shard's power amplifying his strikes and forcing Kaelion to retreat toward the core.

"You can't win," Cyrix said, his voice a mixture of triumph and disdain. "You're weak, Kaelion. You always have been. That's why you failed as a knight. That's why you'll fail here."

Kaelion gritted his teeth, the shard at his side pulsing with a steady, defiant rhythm. "Maybe I am weak. But that's what makes me human."

He lunged forward, his blade catching Cyrix's arm and sending a burst of light through the platform. Cyrix growled in pain, his shard flaring brighter as he retaliated with a vicious strike.

The force of the blow sent Kaelion sprawling, his sword skittering across the platform. He struggled to rise, the weight of the shard pressing against him, the core's energy crackling in the air around him.

Cyrix approached slowly, his expression calm but filled with malice. "You should have stayed in exile. At least then, your failures wouldn't have cost anyone else their lives."

Selara moved before she could think, her shadows surging downward to intercept Cyrix. They struck with the force of a tidal wave, wrapping around him and pulling him back from Kaelion.

Cyrix snarled, his shard glowing violently as he struggled against her attack. "You think you can stop me with tricks and shadows? You're as naive as he is."

Selara's voice was sharp, filled with a mix of fury and desperation. "I'm not trying to stop you. I'm trying to save him."

Her shard flared, the shadows tightening around Cyrix as she pushed her power to its limit. The core responded, its pulsing rhythm growing louder, faster, as the energy in the platform reached a breaking point.

Kaelion forced himself to his feet, his sword heavy in his hand. He glanced at Selara, her form silhouetted against the storm, her shadows coiling around Cyrix like living chains.

"Selara!" he called out, his voice cutting through the chaos. "Don't let it take you!"

Her gaze met his, and for a moment, the shard's whispers faltered. She nodded, her grip on her power steadying as she held Cyrix at bay.

Kaelion turned back to the core, its light and shadow swirling together in a chaotic dance. He stepped toward it, the shard at his side flaring brightly as he raised his sword.

The core's voice echoed in his mind. "Balance demands sacrifice. Will you give what is required?"

Kaelion's grip tightened on the hilt of his blade. "If it means saving her—saving all of us—then yes."

The light of the core surged, engulfing the platform in a blinding brilliance as Kaelion drove his sword into its heart.

Chapter Seventeen: The Shardbearer's Price

The explosion of light and shadow ripped through the platform, an unrelenting storm of energy that consumed everything in its path. Kaelion felt himself lifted off his feet, the world around him dissolving into a kaleidoscope of swirling brilliance. His shard burned against his side, its resonance merging with the chaotic pulse of the Axis's core.

Time seemed to stretch and fracture. Kaelion couldn't tell if seconds or hours passed as the energy surged through him. Whispers filled his mind, their tones shifting between accusatory and pleading.

"Why do you fight us?"

"What will you sacrifice?"

"What remains when the light fades?"

Kaelion clenched his fists, his body trembling under the force of the Axis's voice. "I'll sacrifice whatever it takes. But I won't let this world be consumed—not by the shards, not by Cyrix, not by anything."

The energy around him seemed to hesitate, its chaos slowing into a rhythmic pulse.

"Then prove it."

The light faded, and Kaelion found himself kneeling on the fractured platform. The storm above had quieted, its swirling clouds now circling the core like a watchful eye. The Axis hovered in front of him, its light and shadow spinning in delicate harmony.

But something was wrong.

Selara's voice cut through the stillness, sharp with panic. "Kaelion!"

He turned to see her struggling against Cyrix, her shadows faltering under the overwhelming power of his shard. The older man's expression was twisted with triumph, his shard glowing so brightly it seemed to bleed light into the air around him.

"You think you can stop me?" Cyrix growled, his voice booming with unnatural resonance. "You're nothing but a broken reflection of what this world used to be. I am its future!"

Selara's shadows lashed out one final time, but Cyrix deflected them with a burst of raw energy, sending her sprawling to the ground.

Kaelion's heart clenched as he saw her fall. The shard at his side pulsed violently, its whispers urging him forward.

Kaelion rose, his sword heavy in his hand as he stepped toward Cyrix. The older man turned to face him, his smile filled with mockery.

"Still standing, Kaelion? I'm impressed. But you're too late. The Axis is mine."

Kaelion didn't respond. He raised his blade, its edge glowing faintly in the light of the core.

Cyrix's expression hardened. "You can't stop me. The shards chose me. Their power is mine to wield."

Kaelion's voice was steady, though his body trembled with exhaustion. "The shards didn't choose you, Cyrix. They consumed you."

Cyrix's laughter was cold and hollow. "Then let them consume you as well."

He raised his hand, his shard flaring with blinding light as a wave of energy surged toward Kaelion.

The energy struck, but instead of falling, Kaelion pushed forward, his shard flaring in defiance. He could feel its power coursing through him, its resonance merging with the core's rhythm. The whispers in his mind grew louder, urging him to let go, to surrender fully to the shard's influence.

But Kaelion resisted.

He focused on the memories that grounded him—Liora's voice calling him back during his exile, the quiet strength of Tavriel's guidance, the moments of connection with Selara that had reminded him of his own humanity.

"You don't control me," he whispered, his voice a steel thread in the storm. "I choose what I fight for."

With a final surge of strength, he swung his blade, its light piercing through Cyrix's attack and striking the older man's shard.

The impact sent Cyrix staggering back, his shard cracking under the force of Kaelion's strike. A burst of shadow erupted from the fracture, twisting and writhing as it escaped into the storm. Cyrix cried out, his voice filled with equal parts rage and despair.

"No!" he shouted, his hands clawing at the shard as it splintered further. "This power is mine!"

The shard shattered completely, its pieces dissolving into the air. Cyrix collapsed to his knees, his energy drained, his form flickering like a fading shadow.

Kaelion stepped forward, his sword still raised, his breath ragged.

"It's over, Cyrix," he said.

The older man looked up at him, his eyes filled with a strange mix of fury and sorrow. "You think you've won? The shards don't care who wields them. They will always demand more. And one day, they will consume you too."

Before Kaelion could respond, Cyrix's body dissolved into shadow, his form vanishing into the storm.

Selara rose slowly, her shadows coiling around her as she approached the core. She looked at Kaelion, her expression a mixture of relief and uncertainty.

"You did it," she said softly.

Kaelion nodded, though his eyes remained on the core. "Not yet."

The Axis pulsed faintly, its energy stabilizing as the storm began to dissipate. The platform beneath them grew quiet, the echoes of battle fading into silence.

Tavriel stepped forward, his presence steady as ever. "The Axis waits," he said. "It has tested you, but its final question remains unanswered."

Kaelion turned to him, his brow furrowing. "What question?"

Tavriel's gaze was solemn. "What are you willing to lose to restore balance?"

Kaelion and Selara exchanged a glance, the weight of the question pressing heavily on them both. The shards at their sides pulsed softly, their energy subdued but insistent.

Selara stepped closer to the core, her hand brushing the shard at her neck. "I've already lost so much," she said, her voice trembling. "But if giving this up means saving what's left, then it's a price I'll pay."

Kaelion watched her, his heart aching at the vulnerability in her words. He looked down at his own shard, its glow steady and familiar, and felt the weight of his own choice.

The core pulsed again, its light enveloping them both.

"Then surrender, shard-bearers. And let the Eclipse begin."

Chapter Eighteen: The Eclipse Unleashed

The light of the Axis's core engulfed the platform, swallowing Kaelion and Selara in a vortex of energy that blurred the boundaries between light and shadow. The storm above ceased its howling, replaced by a heavy silence that felt alive with anticipation.

Kaelion felt the shard at his side pull against him, its pulse syncing with the core in a way that made his very essence tremble. The whispers were louder now, not as fragments but as a singular voice filled with purpose.

"Surrender. Only then can balance be restored."

His gaze turned to Selara, her face illuminated by the swirling energies of the core. She clutched the shard at her neck, her shadows flickering around her in chaotic patterns. Her eyes met his, and for a moment, the storm of doubt that had plagued them both seemed to settle.

She nodded, her voice steady despite the trembling in her hands. "Together."

Kaelion gripped his shard and stepped toward the core, its pull growing stronger with each step. "Together."

The platform beneath them cracked as they reached the Axis. Its energy surged outward, weaving ribbons of light and shadow into intricate patterns that encircled them. The shards at their sides grew blindingly bright, their energy resonating with the core in a crescendo that felt as though the world itself was holding its breath.

Kaelion and Selara raised their shards, the energy within them roaring to life.

"Will you surrender what remains of your strength?" the Axis's voice asked, its tone echoing with both command and compassion.

Kaelion's jaw tightened as he felt the shard resist him, its energy clawing at his mind. It whispered promises of power, of control, of salvation without sacrifice. But he knew better now.

"I surrender," he said, his voice firm. "Take it."

The shard shattered in his hand, dissolving into streams of light that flowed into the Axis. Pain lanced through him, sharp and unrelenting, as though a part of himself had been ripped away. His knees buckled, but he remained upright, his resolve anchoring him.

Selara stared at Kaelion, her own shard burning against her chest. She could feel its power coursing through her, a fire that both warmed and consumed. It whispered to her still, its voice soft but insistent.

"You can shape the world," it said. "You can make it whole again, just as you imagined it."

Tears welled in her eyes as she clenched the shard tightly. "No," she whispered. "The world doesn't need to be mine."

With a cry, she ripped the shard from her neck and threw it toward the Axis. It shattered midair, its energy unraveling into threads of shadow that wove themselves into the core.

The pain was immediate and all-consuming, but it brought with it a strange clarity. She fell to her knees beside Kaelion, her breath ragged, but her heart lighter than it had been in years.

The Axis pulsed violently, its energy swirling into a massive, spiraling vortex that engulfed the platform. The light and shadow merged, intertwining in a way that was both chaotic and harmonious. The storm's edge shimmered, its clouds dissolving into streaks of gold and violet that stretched across the sky.

Kaelion and Selara clung to the platform as the energy swirled around them, reshaping the space with a force that was neither destructive nor kind. The core's voice echoed once more, this time softer, almost reverent.

"The balance is restored. The Eclipse begins."

The platform shifted beneath them, its fractures knitting themselves back together. The swirling energy of the Axis began to stabilize, condensing into a brilliant sphere that hovered at the heart of the ridge. The air was quiet now, the oppressive weight of the shards replaced by something softer, something that felt like peace.

Kaelion struggled to his feet, his body aching from the strain of the shard's loss. He looked down at his hands, empty now, but strangely steady.

Selara rose beside him, her shadows gone, replaced by a faint aura of twilight that clung to her like a second skin. She looked at him, her expression unreadable, but her eyes were clear.

"What happens now?" she asked.

Tavriel's voice came from behind them, calm and steady. "Now, the world begins anew."

They turned to see him standing at the edge of the platform, his form bathed in the soft light of the newly formed Eclipse. His shard was gone, its absence leaving him lighter, though his presence was no less commanding.

"The shards were never meant to remain with you," he said. "They were fragments of something greater, meant to guide you to this moment. You have given them back to the Axis, and in doing so, you have allowed the world to heal."

Kaelion looked at the core, its light casting long shadows across the ridge. "Is it over?"

Tavriel's smile was faint, almost wistful. "This chapter is. But balance is not a destination. It is a journey. And the world will need those who understand its cost."

Selara frowned, her hand brushing the empty space where her shard had been. "We gave everything to fix this. What's left for us?"

Tavriel stepped closer, his gaze kind but firm. "What was taken from you has been replaced by something far greater: the freedom to choose your path, unburdened by the shards' influence. The Eclipse is a reflection of that freedom—a reminder that balance is not about perfection, but coexistence."

Kaelion's eyes lingered on the core, its light steady now, its presence no longer oppressive. "And Cyrix?"

Tavriel's expression darkened. "He has chosen his path. But even he is a part of the balance now."

The three of them stood in silence, the weight of their journey settling over them. The storm had passed, and the world felt quieter, gentler, as though it too had been waiting for this moment.

Kaelion turned to Selara, his voice soft but steady. "We did it."

She nodded, her expression softening. "We did."

Tavriel stepped forward, his gaze turning to the horizon. "There is more to be done. The shards may be gone, but the scars of their influence remain. The world will need shepherds to guide it through what comes next."

Kaelion and Selara exchanged a glance, the unspoken question hanging between them.

Finally, Kaelion nodded. "Then we'll do what we can."

Selara smiled faintly, the first true smile he had seen from her in a long time. "Together."

The three of them turned toward the horizon, the light of the Eclipse casting their shadows long across the ridge.

And for the first time in what felt like an eternity, the world was quiet.

Chapter Nineteen: Echoes of the Eclipse

The air was still, the storm's fury replaced by an unfamiliar serenity. The skies above the Twisting Path stretched into a tapestry of violet and gold, the swirling light of the Eclipse casting its soft glow over the shattered ridge.

Kaelion, Selara, and Tavriel descended in silence. The energy of the shards no longer coursed through them, replaced by an absence that felt both liberating and hollow. Each step away from the core brought a strange clarity, as though the chaos that had consumed their lives was finally receding.

Kaelion stopped at the edge of a fractured overlook, his gaze sweeping over the horizon. Below, the Twilight Marches stretched out in endless dusk, their rolling hills bathed in the Eclipse's light. He rested his hand on the hilt of his sword, its weight suddenly foreign without the shard's resonance to anchor him.

"I thought it would feel different," he said, his voice breaking the silence.

Selara stopped beside him, her arms crossed against the chill that lingered in the air. "What did you expect? A parade?"

Kaelion smirked faintly, though his eyes remained on the horizon. "Something like that."

Selara's expression softened as she followed his gaze. "The world doesn't change overnight, Kaelion. We might have stopped Cyrix, but the scars he left—the scars we've all left—don't just fade away."

Tavriel stood a few paces behind them, his presence as steady as ever. The twilight that clung to him seemed softer now, less a shroud and more a mantle. He stepped forward, his voice calm.

"She's right," he said. "The Eclipse is a beginning, not an end. The shards may be gone, but their influence will linger. And the realms will need time to heal."

Kaelion turned to face him, his brow furrowed. "What about us? What's our place in all of this now?"

Tavriel's gaze was distant, his expression thoughtful. "That is a question only you can answer. The shards shaped your path, but they did not define you. Now, you are free to decide who you want to be."

Kaelion's grip tightened on his sword. "It doesn't feel like freedom. It feels... empty."

Selara placed a hand on his shoulder, her touch firm but comforting. "That emptiness is a gift. It means you're finally free of everything that was holding you back. Now you get to choose what fills it."

They continued their descent, the Twisting Path winding back toward the Marches. The air grew warmer as they moved away from the Ridge, though the stillness remained. The echoes of the Axis's energy seemed to fade with each step, leaving only the gentle hum of the Eclipse in the distance.

As they reached the base of the ridge, a group of figures emerged from the shadows of the Marches. Kaelion's hand instinctively went to his sword, but Tavriel raised a hand to stop him.

"It's all right," Tavriel said.

The figures came closer, and Kaelion recognized them as members of the Twilight clans. Their leader, Aelira Sunveil, stepped forward, her staff glowing faintly in the Eclipse's light. Her expression was calm, though her eyes carried a weight of understanding.

"You've done it," she said, her voice reverent. "The Axis is whole again."

Kaelion inclined his head, though his expression was somber. "The Axis is whole, but the world is far from fixed."

Aelira nodded. "True balance is not something that can be imposed. It is something that must be nurtured." She turned to Selara, her gaze softening. "You carry the light of what has been lost. You can help others find their way."

Selara shifted uncomfortably under her gaze. "I don't think I'm anyone's guide, Aelira."

"Perhaps not," Aelira said. "But you are a beacon, whether you wish to be or not."

The clans offered food and shelter, and the trio rested in a small camp nestled within the Marches. The fire crackled softly as the twilight deepened, casting long shadows across the gathered group.

Kaelion sat apart from the others, his sword resting beside him. He stared into the flames, his thoughts tangled in the memories of the battle and the choices he had made.

Selara approached quietly, lowering herself to sit beside him. She didn't speak at first, letting the silence settle between them.

Finally, she broke the quiet. "You're thinking about him, aren't you?"

Kaelion didn't look at her, his eyes fixed on the fire. "Cyrix thought he was saving the world. In his own twisted way, he believed what he was doing was right."

Selara sighed, her gaze dropping to the flames. "Believing you're right doesn't make it true."

"No," Kaelion agreed. "But it makes it harder to see when you're wrong."

They sat in silence for a while longer, the weight of their journey pressing against them.

Tavriel joined them as the fire burned lower, his steps quiet but deliberate. He sat across from them, his gaze thoughtful.

"The Eclipse has given the world a chance," he said. "What it does with that chance is up to those who remain."

Kaelion frowned. "And what about us? Do we just... walk away?"

Tavriel's faint smile returned. "You could. But something tells me your paths aren't done crossing just yet."

Selara smirked. "That sounds suspiciously like a prophecy."

"Perhaps," Tavriel said, his tone light. "Or perhaps just an observation."

As the night deepened, the fire burned down to embers, and the camp grew quiet. Kaelion leaned back, his gaze turning to the sky. The Eclipse hung above them, its light soft and steady, a reminder of what they had fought for.

For the first time in what felt like an eternity, Kaelion allowed himself to hope.

Chapter Twenty: The Light Ahead

Dawn broke across the Twilight Marches, though the sky remained painted in the soft hues of the Eclipse. The once-perpetual dusk of the region seemed warmer now, the golden and violet light blending seamlessly into the land. For the first time in memory, the Marches felt unified, their liminality transformed into a symbol of balance rather than indecision.

Kaelion stood at the edge of the camp, watching as the first stirrings of life awoke around him. The clans moved with a quiet sense of purpose, their steps lighter, their voices filled with cautious optimism. He couldn't help but feel a flicker of envy at their hope—a hope he wasn't sure he shared.

Selara approached, her presence quieter than usual. She carried her cloak draped over one arm, her shadows entirely gone now, leaving her movements oddly unencumbered.

"You're up early," she said, her tone light but probing.

Kaelion glanced at her, his expression unreadable. "Couldn't sleep. Too much on my mind."

She leaned against a nearby tree, crossing her arms. "Still thinking about what's next?"

"Something like that," he said. "We've spent so long chasing the Axis, fighting for balance... and now that it's done, I don't know what comes after."

Selara smiled faintly, though it didn't quite reach her eyes. "You're not the only one. I spent so much time focused on vengeance, on what I lost. Now I'm trying to figure out what's left."

Tavriel appeared, his steps as quiet as ever. He joined them without a word, his gaze fixed on the horizon.

"You always seem to know what's ahead," Kaelion said, his tone half-joking. "Got any prophecies for us this time?"

Tavriel's lips curved into a faint smile. "Prophecies are just possibilities, Kaelion. They show us what might be, not what will be. Your path is yours to decide now."

Kaelion frowned, his grip tightening on the hilt of his sword. "That's the problem. I've spent so long being pulled along by something bigger than myself. I don't know how to just... choose."

Selara touched his arm, her voice softer than usual. "Maybe it's not about choosing the perfect path. Maybe it's just about taking a step and seeing where it leads."

The trio walked to the edge of the camp, where Aelira awaited them. The Twilight shaman stood tall, her staff glowing faintly with the light of the Eclipse. Her expression was serene, but her eyes held the weight of someone who had seen countless struggles and survived them all.

"The clans owe you a great debt," Aelira said, inclining her head toward them. "The balance you restored is fragile, but it is a foundation we can build upon."

Kaelion shook his head. "We didn't do this alone. If anything, we just put the pieces back together. It's up to all of you to make sure they stay that way."

Aelira's smile was kind. "You underestimate the power of what you've done. The Eclipse is not just a symbol—it is a reminder that unity is possible, even in the face of division."

Selara nodded, though her gaze remained distant. "Let's hope the world remembers that."

As they prepared to leave the Marches, the clans gathered to see them off. Aelira stood at the forefront, her staff raised in a silent blessing. The Eclipse's light bathed the gathering in a warm glow, its presence a quiet reminder of what had been won.

Kaelion turned to Tavriel, his brow furrowed. "Where will you go?"

Tavriel's smile was enigmatic. "Where I'm needed. The Eclipse may have begun, but its light must still be guided. There are truths yet to uncover, and questions yet to answer."

Kaelion nodded, though he couldn't help but feel a pang of loss at the thought of their paths diverging.

"What about you?" Tavriel asked, his gaze shifting between Kaelion and Selara.

Selara shrugged, her tone casual but her expression thoughtful. "I'll figure it out. Maybe I'll go back to the Depths, see if there's anything left worth saving. Or maybe I'll find something new."

Kaelion hesitated, his hand brushing the hilt of his sword. "I'll... keep moving. There's still a lot out there that needs fixing."

Tavriel inclined his head. "Then perhaps we will cross paths again. Until then, walk in balance."

The group parted ways at the edge of the Marches, Tavriel disappearing into the distance as Kaelion and Selara continued their journey together. The road ahead was uncertain, the weight of the past still lingering, but for the first time, the path felt open—free of the shards' influence, free of the Axis's pull.

Selara glanced at Kaelion, her smile faint but genuine. "You really think you can fix the world?"

Kaelion smirked, though his eyes remained thoughtful. "Maybe not. But I can try."

They walked on, the Eclipse casting its soft glow over the horizon, a beacon of hope for what lay ahead.

EPILOGUE: SHADOWS OF the Reaver

The Eclipse's light shone faintly over the ruins of the Twisting Path, its gentle hues casting long, eerie shadows across the jagged landscape. All was silent except for the faint hum of residual energy from the Axis's core, its presence a whisper against the stillness.

In the farthest reaches of the ridge, where the storm had once raged most fiercely, a figure stirred.

The space around him seemed fractured, the air rippling as though reality itself struggled to contain his presence. He knelt amid the shattered stone, his form flickering between solidity and shadow.

Cyrix.

His eyes opened slowly, glowing faintly with the fractured light of the shard that had once been his. Though shattered, its remnants clung to him like embers refusing to die, their energy coursing through his veins.

He rose unsteadily, his breath shallow but deliberate. The whispers of the shards were gone, replaced by something colder, more calculating.

"The Axis has shifted," he murmured, his voice quiet but resolute. "But the balance is fragile. They think this is over."

He looked up at the Eclipse, its light steady and unwavering. His lips curled into a faint, bitter smile.

"Balance is just another word for control," he said, his voice hardening. "And control... belongs to those who take it."

With that, he turned and stepped into the shadows, his form dissolving into the darkness.

A Peek at Book Two: The Eclipse Reaver

Two Moons Later

The streets of Solaris Citadel were quieter than usual, the once-bustling city subdued under the Eclipse's strange twilight. Its spires no longer gleamed as brightly, their light softened into something humbler, almost fragile.

Kaelion moved through the crowd, his steps unhurried but purposeful. The people parted for him instinctively, their eyes lingering on the man who had once been their knight and was now something far more uncertain.

He stopped at the edge of the central square, where the Solar Assembly had once held court. The grand platform stood empty now, its golden banners torn and its symbols faded.

"Things have changed," he muttered, his hand brushing the hilt of his sword.

"They always do," a familiar voice replied.

Kaelion turned to see Selara stepping out of the shadows, her cloak pulled tightly around her shoulders. Her eyes were sharp, but there was a hint of weariness in her gaze.

"You're late," he said, though his tone was more amused than reproachful.

"Some of us don't have the luxury of walking through cities unbothered," she replied with a smirk.

Kaelion's expression turned serious. "Have you heard anything?"

Selara nodded, her gaze shifting to the horizon. "Whispers. Rumors of someone gathering power in the Depths. They're calling him the Reaver."

Kaelion frowned, his grip on his sword tightening. "Cyrix."

Selara shrugged, though her expression was grim. "Or someone worse. Either way, it's not going to stop itself."

Kaelion looked out over the city, his thoughts heavy. The balance they had fought so hard to restore was already being tested, its fragility more evident with each passing day.

"Then we stop it," he said finally.

Selara smirked faintly, her shadows flickering around her feet. "You always make it sound so simple."

Kaelion turned to her, his eyes steady. "It's not simple. But it's what we do."

Together, they stepped into the twilight, the light of the Eclipse casting their shadows long across the city.

Also by Kenneth Thomas

The Awakening Thread Chronicles
The Awakening Thread

The Convergence of Minds series
The Digital Agora: A Philosophical Epic of AI and Humanity
Foundation of the Agora
Beyond the Agora: Fractured Realms

The Eclipse Chronicles
Shards of Light

The Veil of Shadows Series
Shattered Dominion
The Fractured Path

Standalone
A Tail of Darkness To Light

The Mirror Within
Echoes of Ink and Heart
Purpose Over Power: The Visionary Path of Servant Leadership
The Questions That Shape Us: Finding Life's Wisdom-The Power of
Inquiry
Where the Shadows Settle
30 Days to Inner Freedom: A Mindful Journey in Addiction Recovery
Towards a Sustainable Future: The UN's 17 Goals
Echoes of Becoming